'As Jess begins to relent and allow Anna to probe into the reasons behind the collapse, her life up until that point is itself uncovered as a spell of sleep, of grief untapped . . . Cole-Adams does not overdo the therapy-speak or psychological inferences in this carefully balanced investigation of a troubled mind'   *Guardian*

'Kate Cole-Adams' accomplished debut traces the slow rehabilitation of a young woman incapacitated, both emotionally and physically, by a mysterious ailment . . . *Walking to the Moon* is a novel of breathtaking lyricism and sensuality. The narrative momentum is faultless, charged with gentle rhythms; pulsations, almost, as if it were bodily. The refined symbolism of water, the moon, caves and the mother figure adds another layer of meaning to this rich mosaic . . . This is a rounded, poignant work. Cole-Adams . . . is a startling new voice'   *Age*

'It's difficult to imagine a novel with a greater degree of narrative integrity, fluent structural intelligence and seemingly effortless power. The prose is accomplished - vivid, but spare . . . this is writing you'd expect from an established novelist . . . This gentle and beautiful novel holds the narrative power of a psychological thriller, but the poetry of its prose is never allowed to blur the focus of its insight, giving hope for a tired old reviewer like me that the notion of literature as a means of raising cultural and social awareness still exists'   Ian McFarlane, *Canberra Times*

'This temporal, contemplative examination of loss and healing rewards slow and careful reading . . . Cole-Adams captures beautifully [the] twilight world that exists somewhere between sleep and wakefulness with language that is so languid, at times it seems lifted from a dream . . . the pieces start to fall quietly into place to celebrate the resilience and recuperation of a woman reclaiming control of her life. The result is deeply rewarding and there are moments of sheer beauty along the way'   *Australian*

Kate Cole-Adams is a Melbourne-based writer and journalist. *Walking to the Moon* is her first novel, and was shortlisted in the Victorian Premier's Literary Awards (Prize for an Unpublished Manuscript) in 2006.

WALKING TO
THE MOON

Kate Cole-Adams

Printed and bound in Great Britain by Clays Ltd, St Ives plc

10 9 8 7 6 5 4 3 2 1

Quercus

First published in Great Britain in 2009 by Quercus
This paperback edition first published in 2010 by

Quercus
21 Bloomsbury Square
London
WC1A 2NS

A CIP catalogue record for this book is available
from the British Library

ISBN 978 1 84916 134 3

Pri... plc

For my parents, Brigid and Peter
And for their parents and theirs before them
All the way back

I

Today I walked. Not just those feeble shuffling steps of recent weeks. Today I walked to the base of the hill I have been watching from my window, and then along the rough clay path that circles it. Although we are high here, and far from the sea, the path has the appearance of worn sandstone and contains, along with pebbles and ground-in eucalypt twigs, tiny fragments of shell. There is a world at my feet. Up close it has the texture of a painting. I crouch for maybe five minutes, maybe fifteen. An ochre passage flanked by platinum-tufted grasses; my eyes move slowly between them: the earth with its coloured fragments and the grasses like hair swept back from a face. Time and I have a new arrangement. We leave each other alone.

As I walk back along the path, the light is gathering among the scribbly gums and a worn, animal smell rises from the cooling earth. A king parrot swoops between the trees, swerving only an arm's length from my face. Its belly is saturated with orange and green. It hangs before me then banks away, following the curve of the earth.

By the time I get back to the nursing home, though, I am cold and heavy and shaking. At the gate I stop and lean against the brick pillars. The path across the garden seems impossible. Steff sees me first and sets out across the grass, shaking her head.

'Unbelievable,' she mutters when she is close enough for me to hear. 'Bloody unbelievable.'

I put my arm around her shoulder, too tired to speak or hold thoughts, and we move slowly, slowly towards the house. Steff doesn't know how to treat me now. She used to call me sleeping beauty. Now she calls me nothing.

'Bloody unbelievable,' she says again, when we get upstairs to my room. 'Sit. Arms. Thermometer. Lie down.'

Then she is gone. As I lie on my side in bed the shivering resolves itself into a slow rhythmic pulse, as if my organs—stomach, kidney, spleen—are clenching darkly on the beat: cold, cold, cold.

The next day I cannot get up. There is no question of even trying. It is not pain. It is more a physical preoccupation, the body taken up entirely with itself. It is a negation of movement. Matter, anti-matter; movement, anti-movement. As if a heavy cloak has been laid upon me.

Steff waits until the younger of the doctors arrives before speaking. 'I found her staggering outside in the cold yesterday afternoon. Nearly broke my back getting her up here. Didn't tell any of us she was going, and now she won't eat anything.' She stands looking at the doctor expectantly.

The doctor, who has a round face and sandy hair that he combs back with some sort of oil, looks at me mildly and says, 'Let's see now.' He looks in my eyes and ears, checks my blood pressure and temperature, turns away, folding the tourniquet. 'I'll pop back tomorrow,' he says, heading for the corridor.

'She won't eat,' says Steff again, accusingly, as he opens the door. She says it as if I'm doing it deliberately. Won't eat. Won't get well. 'Try to eat,' says the mild doctor, turning back briefly. I nod and close my eyes.

'Un-fuckin'-believable,' says Steff when he has gone. She says it to him, not me. Steff only talks to me through a third person. As if she is afraid of sickness.

A heavy cloak has been laid upon me.

It is a forgettable little hill in a forgettable little suburb at the outer edge of town, where housing developments leach into wetlands of migratory birds and across the fields where children once rode ponies. Here the plains that stretch west from Sydney give way to mountains, and the sprawl contracts to a seam of tourist towns that follow the rail line up the sandstone plateaux and cling to the great escarpment I saw as a child.

At first they had me in a hospital in town. When I didn't get better, they sent me here. My husband keeps trying to get me moved back to the city, somewhere with people my own age where I can get what he calls proper help. But Hil wants me here.

'We need to get her sap flowing again,' she said to the owner, Viv, not long after I first woke up.

'Your niece,' said Viv, glancing towards me, 'doesn't have any sap to flow. Not yet. Leave her with me. We'll do what we can.'

Twice a week Hil catches the train from Central Station. It takes her an hour and ten minutes to get here. 'Soon as you're strong enough we'll get you out of here, hey Jess? You know there's a room at my place if you want. Just got to get you on your feet first.'

Slow syrup. Today I will not sit up or look out of the window above my bed. Today I will lie. The late-morning sun slants through the silver birch on to my pillow. I close my eyes, and the shifting dapples settle inside me. There is nothing to regret.

It is just a bump really, my little hill. A child's curved line. It sits on the other side of the oval, rising above its circle of gums. A mound the developers forgot.

Steff comes back before lunch, bringing Tina. Together they manoeuvre me into a wheelchair and push me through to the wash-room. Inside, I stand shakily and hold on to a steel rail while Tina helps me remove my clothes. There is a plastic stool in the shower alcove and I lower myself on to it clumsily, without grace.

'Back where she started,' says Steff. She checks the temperature of the spray from the hose before pointing it at the small of my back. 'Six weeks since she woke up and she's back to square one.'

'Not really,' says Tina, pulling latex gloves over fingernails sealed in clear polish. 'It's just a setback. She'll be right in a few days. But it wasn't such a brilliant idea, was it, taking off on your own?' This addressed to me, as she raises my left wrist and smooths anti-bacterial body wash into my armpit. She's like a sleek bird, Tina, with her tiny wrists and ankles and her precise movements. Her skin is very pale and her hair dark and cut very short, and there is a single gold ring in her nose. Watching her gives me pleasure. I try to gather my face into a wry smile for her. Reduced, I can feel

6

the effort in every muscle, the intricate system of ropes and pulleys required for each expression. A lopsided flutter. Too hard.

'Hil's going to be really impressed,' says Steff.

The hardest thing—harder than balancing as I pull on my jeans, harder than the old-woman shuffle to the bathroom, harder than making my way step by step down to the dining room—the hardest thing is to speak. Even listening sends a grey tide through my body: the arrangement of words and phrases and sentences, balanced upon and within each other; the dead ends and digressions, each requiring energy; the slow accumulation of meaning. Tracking it exhausts me.

In a vase next to my bed are the flowers Hil brought earlier in the week, a cluster of greeny-yellow banksias from home and a broken-off twig of birch taken from the garden.

'Don't let Viv see you nicking stuff from her garden,' warned Tina, only half joking.

Curled again on my side, it is the leaves that now draw my gaze, not the flowers, which seem too bright and upstanding. The tip of the nearest leaf is already turning brown, like wrapping paper. I dwell in sickness, I think to myself. And then, no, not sickness: illness. Dwell and ill. Watery words. Pool. I think of a leaf in cool dark water, and of all the other bits of life that accumulate there and sink. Stems, stamen, antennae, eyes, each dismantled cell by cell by swarms of blind microbes, taken in, transformed, released. The way my mother's hair rose around her that day in the lake, how the cicadas fell silent, the blood booming in my ears like wing beats.

How one day last year I lay down and couldn't get up.

I am in bed this time for four days. My temperature rises and my glands swell, and my body is reconfigured into planes of sensation. Discomfort, Viv calls it, and perhaps she is right; it is not comfortable. But it is peaceful in its way. I lie on my side and my breath comes out in small moans. It is easier than silence. Each breath is made of air and water and warmth, and I send them out like tiny rafts, carrying away the excess.

The nursing home is on the city side of the oval in the highest part of the suburb. It was first opened as a hospice for dying Victorians, the 'home for the incurables', then, after the foundations gave way, rebuilt in the forties of blond brick with darker bricks around the windows, and curved nautical corners. The place still sits on its original grounds, as Viv likes to say, though really it's just a garden, with a couple of birches and an elm that seems to be sickening and a few spindly azaleas Viv tends without much success.

'Soil's fucked,' says Steff, whose dad's a market gardener and knows about acid. Most of the garden is taken up by a pine the height of a small office block that clogs the ground with slippery impermeable needles and blocks the sun from about three o'clock.

It is a private nursing home, slightly worn, but well built. I like it. I like its bland colours, its thick plaster, its steadfastness. I like the unassuming brass plaque by the front entrance, announcing its official opening in 1947. I like it because it feels familiar. I feel as if I have been here before.

Viv has been here for a long time. Some doctors (my husband included) mistrust her because she encourages 'complementary' approaches such as acupuncture. Not that you would think it to meet her. She wears high, bright sandals and dark eye makeup and pulls her eternally russet hair back each day in a perfect French roll. Tina calls her the madam, though not to her face.

Tina also insists that Viv is a medium. Once a month, she says, Viv holds a séance at her house in the next suburb, and sometimes even invites the relatives of people who have died at the nursing home. She doesn't charge, says Tina, who maintains that Viv has told her all this herself. Tina says she has also heard (not from Viv) that the person she is really looking for is her son, who walked out of their home one morning twenty years ago, when he was seventeen, and never came back. Tina drops her voice as she repeats this although the only other people in the room are Steff and me, and I am pretending not to listen. Steff makes a harrumphing sound. But Tina is adamant. Viv has never been able to contact him, she says, and his body has never turned up, so she still hopes he might be alive. Maybe, she adds with a shrug, he just didn't want to come home. Steff says nothing, but her wide face becomes still and set.

9

Either way, there are movement and meditation classes advertised on the notice board and tai chi in the mornings, along with weekly sessions of art and music therapy, none of which I attend. I am here because Viv is an old school friend of Hil's, and because she knew my mother.

'Bloody sanitarium,' says Steff.

A week or so after I woke up I took the curved stairway, step by shuffling step, downstairs to the library. There is a lift for wheel-chairs in the new wing at the back of the building, but the rest of us are encouraged to walk, when we can. 'Healthy body, healthy mind,' says Viv. 'I make no apologies for being old-fashioned.'

'She makes no apologies for anything,' says Steff.

It is a small room, with a fluorescent strip light and no windows. It may once have been part of the dining room next door. The light shows up the cracks in the upper reaches of the paintwork and the peeled back covers of books. Beneath the room's surface is the weary, comforting smell of old paper. The lower shelves are filled mainly with magazines and games: *Women's Weekly*, Ludo, a chess set with no knights. Above them in rows and stacks are Dick Francis, Colleen McCullough, H.E. Bates, Shere Hite: a muddle of books, linked only by their inscriptions: To Dad, get well soon, love mum and the kids; To my darling Aggie, be brave, 1951. Higher up are what Viv calls the more intellectual books: a bible, a Roget's Thesaurus, a medical dictionary without a cover.

You only have to be unconscious for six hours and they call it a severe brain injury. If you don't wake up in two weeks it's a pro-longed coma. And after that they start thinking about moving you out of the hospital into rehab, or somewhere like here. 'Three weeks you were out,' said Tina, 'then they brought you here and you woke up, just like that, on Boxing Day.' There is a wooden stool behind the library door with steps that can be folded away underneath. By the time I had dragged it, climbed, balanced and reached above me for the dictionary, my arms were shaking and I was cold again inside. I lowered myself carefully and perched on the stool, shuddering, until my body came back into focus. 'You're one of the lucky ones,' said Tina. 'You'll be ready to go home soon. Back to your real life.'

I sleep, I wake, barely touching the sediment before pushing off again lightly with my foot.

'Overdid it a bit, eh Jess?' Hil is sitting on the chair beside me when I open my eyes, legs stretched out in front of her. I raise my eyebrows a little and shrug. 'Sleep,' she says. And I do.

The next day, though, my body will not let me be. My skin is hot and taut and cold, and every position is not right. Curled on either side, my hips grind into the mattress and the sheets rub my skin. On my back, even with the blankets pulled tight around my neck, my belly and chest are adrift, washed by icy spasms. The doctor comes again, and pushes my tongue down with a wooden spatula. 'Say aah.' My tonsils are up. He says I probably got a chill on my walk. Nothing too serious. But he gives me antibiotics and something for the fever.

Viv pops in on her daily tour. 'Just poking my nose in. Really darling, you'll never get well if you keep gallivanting off into the hills. Whatever were you thinking?'

Every day at about eleven a flock of pigeons enters the sky outside my window. I never notice them arrive, I just look and they are there, an eddy of birds circling my hill. I never see them go, either, or think about them, until it is mid-morning again and they are back.

'Anna Greene is dropping in to see you this morning,' says Tina. She releases the blind too quickly, so that the string spins around the top and she has to take off her shoes and climb on the end of my bed to unwind it.

'Who's Anna Greene?'

'You'll like her. She's meant to be very good.'

I don't like her: she is perfect. Pale hair cropped around her face in soft tufts; cotton drawstring pants in a neutral, unbleached colour. Biscuit or taupe or whatever they call it where she does her shopping. Hil would call it beige. A loose, white, short-sleeved shirt. Deep blue beads around her neck. She pulls up a chair uninvited and sits at the foot of my bed, one leg tucked beneath her. Mid-forties. Fifty. I can't tell. With her flat Italian sandals and her quiet textured voice.

'Your aunt, Hil, asked me to come and see you. She thought

it might be helpful.'

'Are you another doctor?'

'I'm a therapist. But I also work with the body.'

'Hil didn't tell me she'd spoken to you.' As soon as I say it I wish I hadn't. I don't want this Anna Greene to know.

She has very blue, very pale eyes, and whenever I glance at her she is looking straight at me.

'It must be strange being here with most of the others so much older.'

'I don't mind. I'm not really up to talking much.'

'The matron, Viv, says you came here from the hospital.'

'That's right.'

'Do you remember much about the hospital?'

'No.'

'You were very sick.'

I turn my head towards the window, through which the pigeons, fewer than usual, are spiralling beneath low, buckled clouds. 'I don't remember.'

'How are you feeling? How have you been going recently?'

It is hard not to look at her. She has pulled one knee up to her chest and wrapped the other around it so that she is almost curled in the chair. She is like a big, blonde cat, loose-limbed and satisfied.

'Okay. Pretty tired still.'

She nods and says nothing. I look back out through the window towards the birds, but they are gone. Just like that. And after a while the fact of her sitting there, watching me, is too much.

'These birds come every day at the same time,' I say at last, still looking out the window. 'And then they go.'

'What sort of birds?'

'Pigeons.'

'Someone probably owns them,' she says. 'They probably let them out for exercise.'

I hadn't thought of that. And now I am upset. She has taken away the mystery; she has put my birds in a context, so that they are not even my birds any more. They are someone else's. They come from somewhere and go back there, to cages. They haven't even chosen the spot in which they fly. I stare at the ceiling. For a moment I think I am going to cry.

'That's just a guess,' she says, trying to keep her voice neutral. She has realised her mistake. 'I don't know where the birds come from. Do you suppose they could be wild?'

'No.'

She is silent again, everything off to a bad start. Her predicament gives me a sudden little jab of satisfaction.

Illness pares you away: manners, appetite, ego, past.

Shell, membrane, albumen. Until all that remains is the smooth gold yolk.

'Is it all right if I sit here?' says Anna Greene.

I glance back towards her, shrug. 'Suit yourself.'

'Yes, I will.' She pauses. 'But what do you want?'

'I just want to get out of here.'

She nods, and waits, and when I don't speak, she says, 'I could help you if you'd like.'

I shrug again, but I don't look away.

'The only thing is, if that's what you want, you will have to let me know.' After a while, when I don't speak, she says. 'Or perhaps you don't know what it is that you want.'

'Yes,' I say at last. 'I don't know.'

'So maybe we'll talk a little more now.'

'Are you a psychiatrist?'

'My background is in psychology, but these days I work also with the body—sometimes with exercises, sometimes with touch. I run an exercise class,' she says. 'Downstairs in the rec room, every Tuesday at eleven. It's nothing strenuous. More a way of getting back into your body. Helping you find your body again. You might like to come and try it out. People find it very beneficial.'

'I might do that,' I say, and nod, careful. Might. Might not.

'What about you?' she says. 'Can you tell me a bit about what you are doing here?'

'There's not much to tell. I just got sick one day.'

'Sick how?'

'Headache. I had a headache, and I was feeling nauseous and dizzy.'

'What happened then?'

'Then I lay down.'

'Do you remember anything about the coma?'

'No. I was unconscious.'

'Some people do have memories. At least images. Impressions. I know one woman who thought she was climbing the tree that had been in her back yard when she was a child. She was unconscious for two weeks. She could describe every twig, the bark on every branch.'

'What happened when she got to the top?'

'She wasn't trying to get to the top. She climbed as far as the tree house where she used to hide when she'd had enough. And she stayed there until she felt ready to come down.'

'Well I don't remember a thing. It was an infection; a bacterial infection. Ask the doctors. Ask Hil. I'm sure you already have.'

Memory. Anti-memory. I remember waking. That is all. I woke into the dark, and I thought I was dead.

'The doctors think you might have had a form of meningitis, but they're not sure.'

'Right. Thank-you.' After a while I add, 'You can always tell the coma patients. They've all got the same scar.' And I touch my throat lightly, at the base, where they put the breathing tube in when I was unconscious.

'Tracheotomy.' She nods and smiles slightly.

'Yes, it's our badge of honour. We're always checking out everyone's necks around here. One woman downstairs has had hers for nearly twenty years, and you can still see it.'

'Does that worry you?'

'The scar? No. I like it.'

'You like it. What is it that you like about it?'

'I don't know. Not what you think. It keeps me company.'

'What do you think I think?'

'I don't know. You know. Let's talk about something else. I'm tired.'

'What do you want to talk about?'

'Nothing.'

*

I woke from nothing into nothing. Nameless. I opened my eyes and closed them. Open. Closed. Nothing. But the words stayed in my body. Close. Open. And after a while the flickering darkness rearranged itself into slabs and passages, and I felt that I was in a small stone chamber which was an anteroom to a far greater chamber, and that in that other room was life, or death. I could not tell which. It was quite matter of fact. I had to decide whether to go there. There was nothing mystical or even mysterious about it. It was familiar. Like brushing up against someone you've sat next to all your life, and never noticed.

It was only when I tried to move that I panicked. I felt cables from my throat, my wrist, between my legs. The world slipped and the separation was so vast I had to drag my spreading self into a pin-prick of focus to find me again. I traced my outline from the inside. Starting at the right thumb and moving through my body I pushed myself into each digit, each limb, the small of my back, the space between my eyes. Fighting my way back to that fragile, glistening strand. I am the smallest, most delicate of spiders caught in the suck of the wind and below me my web hangs geometric and precise. I woke into blackness. No bedside lamp or radio or voice or shaky cigarette. I woke into blackness. Without.

The next time I came awake, it was day, caramel light, a voice nearby. I'm still not sure whose, a woman's though. I heard the voice and I thought about opening my eyes, and I didn't. All that day, and the next.

On the third day, the specialist from the hospital arrived on his weekly rounds, while I was sleeping, and woke me by sticking a needle in my foot. I think I swore.

'That's more like it,' he said.

And then someone, Steff it might have been, said, 'Well, she's taken her time.'

I kept my eyes shut, heart crowding my chest. The doctor tried a few more needles, one in my other foot, a couple in my arms, testing for responses. I lay very still, trying to slow my breathing. Then he said, 'Just a moment, I'll try something else,' and the next thing I felt his fingers at my eye, smelled the disinfectant soap on him, and then I was looking straight into my own face. Just a moment. The reflected blue rim of the eye, the sloping lid pulled back by his fingers, and then I rolled my pupils back up into the darkness of my head and waited until he stopped. I heard him writing something on paper, packing his things into his bag—notes, needle, mirror—clicking it shut, crossing the room to the door.

'You can tell her family she's awake,' he said on his way out.

I am the youngest of the patients here, though Viv calls us residents. In the room next to mine is Irena. Mrs Ivanovich. Irena fell off a horse five years ago, having a riding lesson with her daughter. Now she lies propped in her bed smiling kindly at everyone who passes. 'Hello Mrs Ivanovich, how are you today?' says Steff in her hearty voice.

'Not too bad thank-you Stephanie. Not too bad. Yourself?'

Her husband visits on Saturdays and sometimes brings the kids, though less often now that they're getting older. 'It's too hard for them,' says Tina. Especially the eldest, a girl of around thirteen. Sometimes I see them from my window as they get out of the car. All in their nice clothes, the girl's shoulders hunched forwards, head down, chewing on a strand of long dark hair. Mr Ivanovich leaves his jacket folded in the car and checks himself quickly in the side window, then puts his arm around the girl's shoulders and propels her gently up the path while the boy runs ahead with the flowers.

The boy gets up first, taking the stairs in twos, then pauses for a moment outside her door, slowing his breath before going in. 'Hello Mama.' I hear them from my room. 'Hello my love. Give me a kiss. Careful where you sit.' He can't sit though; only for those moments before the others arrive. Then he's moving around the room, picking up trays, pressing buttons, pulling the curtain around her bed back and forth along its rail, until his dad snaps at him and Irena remonstrates softly. 'It's all right Sergei, let him go.' The boy spends the rest of the time in the garden. He has a special place at the bottom of the pine tree. He pulls his knees up and wraps his arms around them and waits.

Tina says it's best if the kids don't come, even the boy. 'It just upsets her. Puts her out for a couple of days.'

Normally the door to her room is open when I pass. 'Hello Irena.'

'Hello darlink.' She speaks softly as if her voice is full of air. 'You are walking good now, Jess. Good gel.' The huge dark eyes of a calf. When she is excited she wobbles her head from side to side on her pillow. That is all she can move. When her husband leaves at the end of his visit, she asks him to draw the curtains around her bed and they stay pulled shut for the rest of the day. Sunday too. If anyone tries to talk to her she closes her eyes, squeezes them shut until they go away.

Many of the people here are stroke patients. Strokes. 'Stroke in room four', or 'room thirteen stroke', or sometimes it's just a number. 'Bedpan in eight', 'visitor for two'. At the other end of the corridor there's an overdose, and downstairs a couple of car accidents. Prangs, Steff calls them. A few doors down from Irena there's a drowning, or near enough. A middle-aged man who once ran a sporting goods store. He left his Randwick home one afternoon, told his wife he was going to buy cigarettes and washed up a couple of hours later at Bondi. 'Tried to top himself, I bet,' says Tina. 'Insurance.' You never see his wife, or his kids. Just his mother, who comes on Wednesdays. She is very distinguished, grey hair pulled up in a loose, elegant bun, and trouser suits made of fine wool or linen. She sits by his bed until hours are over, stroking his face with the backs of her fingers. Sometimes she takes a pair of folding scissors from her handbag and cuts his hair.

Once after she had gone I thought I heard him call out, a thick bellowing. When I looked in, though, he was lying on his back, quite still, just his hands on his chest moving vaguely. Like kelp.

I call him the swimmer.

One evening, as I pass Irena's door on my way to bed, she calls to me. 'Here darlink, here Jess.'

'Over here, close now,' she urges as I stand in the doorway, clicking her tongue until I reach her bedside. 'Good gel. Now, you are small. You lie next me.'

'Um. I don't think I'll fit Irena. Would you like me to get Tina?' My voice trails off. 'Or someone?' She rolls her eyes at my confusion, and rocks her head. 'Quick. Quick. You fit. Only take moment.'

Eventually I sit beside her and begin to lower myself on to my side, facing her.

'No. No. Not look at me, silly gel. Look up. Up.'

There is a galaxy on the ceiling. Stars, planets, fluorescent constellations, a crescent moon. Close like this she smells of biscuits or rice. Warm grain. I take a deep breath and let it out slowly.

'See Jess,' she says. 'My husbant is make me a sky.'

On Mondays and Fridays, Hil catches the train from Central, then walks the twenty-five minutes from the station to the nursing home. 'Hey Jess.' She has never learned to drive and doesn't intend to. 'What's wrong with legs?'

What was wrong with the industrial revolution, I complain, and she shrugs. 'I use what I need, Jess, no point needing more.' She won't use a computer either, although she always carries a mobile phone. Four nights a week, she rings me from the Dump, the youth centre she runs for the church out of the old hall around the corner from her place. She has been doing it ever since I remember.

When I was sixteen I moved into her house in Bondi while I did my HSC. Every morning at six-thirty she would wake me and we would pull on shorts or tracksuit pants and T-shirts and set off along the path cut into the sandstone cliffs between Bondi and Bronte. There the city lost its grip. The land pushed through and the suburbs stretching inland were just a thin skin waiting to be peeled back. At that hour everything had purpose. Dogs on leads dragging their owners. Fishermen pushing bits of squid on to hooks. Couples pacing each other through the apricot light. Hil and I would walk without talking, pushing hard against the inclines, almost running the down-slopes. Hil striding ahead on the thick muscles of her thighs. Me, grumbling at first, hacking away the tightness of the night's cigarettes, feeling the sweat begin to prickle my armpits, the slight nausea. And then release; the body loosening, gliding slip-easy into its own rhythm and the breeze at my face and light leaping from the sea. My warm breath and the day.

When I was younger, I used to love taking friends to visit her. Her walls were covered with things to look at: posters in foreign languages, wall hangings from Timor, a copper calendar from Nepal. My room, the room where I used to sleep, looked on to the pathway that runs along the side of the house. The wooden fence separating her place from the one next door was long gone beneath layers of bougainvillea and honeysuckle and in the morning, if you stuck your head out, all you could smell was green. The weatherboard in my room was unplastered, painted a pale, pale yellow that I had picked out when I moved in. We did it in an afternoon, and the eggshell blue trim around the windows, and when we were done Hil opened a bottle of sparkling apple juice and we sat on the paint-dotted sheets on the floor and raised our glasses and she said, 'Well Jess, here's to the present.'

At the youth centre she hands out condoms to kids as young as twelve. The church that owns the hall has forbidden it, but Hil lists them as 'miscellaneous' in her monthly accounts and everybody pretends she means biscuits. Later, after the Dump closes at ten or eleven, she sets off on foot, feeling her way across vacant blocks, crawling into barricaded squats. In her satchel she carries a phone, food, clean fits. Sometimes she brings news of empty beds in nearby hostels or shelters. Sometimes she holds their bird bodies against her strong one until the ambulance comes. Most often she just chats, passes on messages from absent parents or parole officers, gives details of court appearances, the use of her phone. In the mornings she finds offerings outside the front door of her leaning weatherboard: notes under stones, flowers from other people's gardens.

When she was at school, a teacher told Hil that what she lacked in good looks she made up for in personality. Hil laughs. She says being plain has its advantages. I like the way she looks. Just a face. Hazel eyes, cleft chin, freckles. Hil. When she is old she will be handsome. I am not the only one to see it. Men propose but she always turns them down. She has never had a boyfriend—or a girlfriend as far as I know.

'I'm not a virgin, Jess, if that's what you're worried about,' she told me once. 'I'm just not interested.'

'But what about...I mean you must get...Don't you ever...?'

'Wank? No. Tried it once but I fell asleep. I'm just not, Jess. That's all there is to it. Better talk about your sex life if we want some excitement.'

But that was a long time ago. I was living then with my friend Emma in a skinny blue terrace in Darlinghurst. She had black hair and red lips and we went to university and waitressed or sold books or clothes, or whatever people wanted us to sell, or cleaned houses (other people's), and then went dancing. We danced a lot and drank a lot and there were men with dirty fingernails at the breakfast table, and once they had gone there was Emma and me curled up in her queen-sized bed with tea and toast with honey, comparing notes or consoling one another.

Sometimes when it all got too much I would pack my bag and take the bus to Bondi, to Hil's and stay there for a night or two where it was peaceful and the sun through the window settled in ragged patches on my single bed. The key was by the back door and she never asked questions. One day I just moved back in.

She is thinner than she looks, Hil, undressed. In the shower the skin of her belly stretches very pale between her wide-set, protruding hip bones. The water runs in ropes between her small round breasts, the pink nipples, across the smoothness of her stomach and into her fine, reddish-brown pubic hair. Her body is a puzzle; the ruddy, freckled face and workman's arms against the smooth, milky torso.

Tina told me that once, in that week before I awoke, she came into my room and Hil was crying. Hil would never tell me that. Or that she read me books or talked to me or massaged my body with oil. These things do not surprise me, but I cannot imagine them either. I want to know what she said to me. I want to know if she thought I would die, but not enough to ask her.

It makes me feel funny, the thought of her sitting next to me, crying. It is a dark thick feeling, without words. Sometimes after Hil goes the feeling builds up around me, and I cannot find a place where it is not. Sometimes I wish she did not visit as much. Even when she doesn't say anything—even when we just sit, or play backgammon, or chat about other things—after she goes the feeling is there.

One day I tell her it's okay if she only comes once a week.

'Don't worry about it,' she says. She is standing with her back to me in my bed, leaning out the window on her elbows.

'But Hil, it's nearly six hours out of your day, and I'm so much better now, I'll be out of here soon. Viv said.'

'And?'

'Nothing. Nothing. I just don't want you to go to all this effort.'

She has turned, and is facing me, bum resting on the window ledge. 'No effort.' She shrugs lightly.

'No, I just—' I shrug back.

'You want me to come once a week, I'll come once a week.'

She pulls herself to standing, pats down the back of her jeans, then into the silence she adds: 'You can't stay here forever, mate.'

'No one's suggesting—'

'And you can't keep getting sick every time Viv says you're ready to leave.'

'I didn't—that's not fair.' My throat tightens around the feeling of 'not fair'. There is a prickling behind my eyes; my neck and face suddenly hot. I look away from Hil, twist my neck around to stare out through the window next to my bed. The sky is empty, free of birds.

'C'mon Jess, buck up. It's not the end of the world.'

There are differing views as to what is, or has been, wrong with me. The doctors at the hospital in town agreed finally to put my collapse down to an undiagnosed infection, though even that was uncertain. One specialist came all the way out to the nursing home a week after I awoke, bringing a colleague, to examine me again, for what he called his own satisfaction. The colleague asked a lot of questions about my family, none of which seemed very relevant, and which after a while seemed to set up a swaying motion inside me and then a sick dizziness so that I closed my eyes, and when Hil arrived soon after, she asked them to leave.

What seems clearer is that my recovery in the slow weeks since then has not been what was hoped for. I have had blood tests and stool tests and brain scans; I have had injections of vitamins C and B. I have been told to stay in bed and to get out of it. What has remained constant has been a lassitude verging at times on paralysis, and, until recently, an inability—Steff calls it a refusal—to walk. Mostly I feel tired.

In the midst of this I have turned away the few visitors, my husband among them, who have made the trip to this outermost suburb to offer me comfort or company. I have told staff not to put calls through to my room, and nor have I answered most of the letters or cards that have accumulated in the bottom drawer of the dresser by my bed. I will only see Hil.

At the same time I am bored. I am bored with sickness, its strictures and relentless needs. I am bored with the dullness in my body, the wasted space, the finite allotment of energy. On Tuesday at eleven, I make my way down to the rec room. When I open the door there are three old women in their tracksuits, and Anna Greene at the front of the room. 'Come in, Jess,' she says and smiles. The three old women all turn around expectantly. Maud says, 'Hail the queen of Sheba.'

'Come in,' Anna says again, 'and take your shoes off. We'll just do a warm-up.'

Harder now to leave than to do as she says. I put my shoes by the wall and find myself a spot at the back. Closest to the door.

'Now,' says Anna. 'I want you to stand with your feet hip width apart, close your eyes—or open, Elsie, if that helps with your balance—and feel your feet against the floor. Good, and just breathing. Breathing is always good. Best not forget.'

A giggle from Maud. I keep my eyes shut, unamused.

'You too, Jess,' says Anna. 'Allow your body breath. Allow the soles of your feet to feel the floor. Relax your buttocks. Bending your knees slightly. Letting your arms hang loose, Maud. And now

29

start jiggling from the knees. That's right, Mary. Stay loose. Shaking your body down like a sack of grain. All over. Not just the outside bits. The inside parts too. Relax the jaw. Let your jaw drop open Jess, don't worry what it looks like. And sound. Sigh it out with the breath. Ah-ah-ah-ah.'

I open my eyes and there she is, standing in front of us, jaw hanging open, looking stupid, shaking these ugly sounds out of herself. The old women join in, one by one. Mary's hair falling out of its bun, Maud's breasts bumping against her stomach. Ah-ah-ah-ah. Sometimes bursting into laughter, all of them together, ah-ah-ah. I keep my legs straight, straight-faced, little bobs from the thighs. Policeman plod; 'ello 'ello 'ello.

'C'mon love,' says Maud, catching my eye. 'We all look stupid. You don't want to stand out.'

I roll my eyes, pull a face at her and keep bobbing. Anna ignores me. Eventually I start to loosen, feeling the rhythm of the movement in my heels and the balls of my feet; my stomach and arms and jaw. I keep my eyes closed, let my throat open, let the sounds bump out until I too find myself releasing a quick laugh. A child in a car on a corrugated road. Ah-ah-ah. After a while Anna tells us to slow, then stop, then stand with our eyes shut, and feel how it is in our bodies. Then we sit down on chairs, and she asks us how we felt when we were standing still. Elsie says she feels a bit funny in her tummy, but nothing to worry about. Mary's knees feel big. Maud can't stop laughing. I say my legs feel heavy, weird, as if there is nothing holding them up.

'Would you like to lie on the ground, here,' Anna says. Not really a question. I shrug, then get up and lie in front of her. She sits at my side on the floor, cross-legged. 'What I'm going to do,' she says, 'is to put my hands beneath your knees, like this.'

Her hands feel very warm through my pants. Very solid. Surprising somehow. Not unwelcome. Not even embarrassing.

'Just let your knees relax,' says Anna, 'and remember to breathe.'

I take a deep slow breath, and feel my legs, one then another, regain their focus.

'That's good,' says Anna. 'Just let those legs know they have some support.' And suddenly, shockingly, I am crying. Sad creaky hiccoughs.

I roll away from her, on to my side. Anna leaves a hand resting on my thigh for a moment, then takes it away as I pull myself to sitting, puts a hand on the back of my neck while I slump forward.

'Is that all right?' she asks. 'That I touch you?'

I nod, quiet my breathing, feel the relief of her hand cupped behind my neck, then shake my head abruptly, shake her off.

'Jess?'

I keep shaking my head.

'Jess, come back. Look at me.'

I look up. Her face is big, close, her eyes are blue, dreamlike, and I am leaving through the back of my head, shrinking into a pinprick of dark light behind me. For a moment, I stop hearing, cocooned, untouchable.

And then the lilt of her voice again, even, persistent.

'Come back, Jess. Bring yourself back. Look at me, Jess.'

It is like waking. Nothing dramatic. Just finding myself back, her eyes the anchor. She is squatting in front of me, solid, unthreatening. The room seems bigger than before, and there is an odd sense of space around me. I move my head slowly from side to side. I almost smile. She nods.

31

'That's good work. You've done a lot. It's a good idea to rest now. Go and have a sleep.'

As I leave from the rec room a few minutes later, she catches up with me in the corridor. 'Jess, I meant to say, I see private clients in that room over there twice a week, Tuesdays and Fridays. I've got a space free on both days. If you'd like.'

One day Maud's daughter comes to visit at lunchtime and brings her child. Maud's fourth grandchild. 'Breeders, aren't we?' Maud laughs and pushes her chair back from the table. Her daughter, Carol, places the child in Maud's wide lap, and it pushes itself to standing while Maud holds it around the chest, pulling faces at it, making noises. The child's fat little legs work her knees like dough. It reaches towards her and grabs at her glasses with one hand. 'Oi. Carol. Give us a hand. That's my last pair.' Carol leans and takes the glasses from the child, unwraps its fingers from around the arm. The child turns its attention back to Maud, stretches its fingers for her nose, pats around her eyes with its small fat hands. I am at the next table, still sitting, though lunch is cleared away. The sun is coming in through the window and I watch them for a while before returning to the magazine I am pretending to read.

'Give Jess a hold. She'll like a hold.'

I look up when I hear my name. Viv is at the next table now, arms extended for the blue-clad infant. She raises it to her shoulder, gives a firm, brisk jiggle, which does not seem to upset the child, who reaches immediately for her glasses. 'Oh no you don't.'

'Jessica,' she calls. I have glanced down again at my magazine, and look up reluctantly, knowing what it coming.

'Here you are. This is Joshua.' And she plonks him abruptly

on the table in front of me, bum on top of *New Idea*.

'Hello Joshua.' Joshua stares at me with an impartial, appraising expression. He does not reach for me. I hold my hands on either side of his solid, hot body. Viv has moved back to the other table, but I am sure she is looking to see how I go. The baby and I regard each other. I realise I am barely breathing, and then that I am a little afraid. I breathe deeper, bring my face a fraction closer to his. It is a sweet, rich smell, the smell of babies. Not unpleasant, despite the hint of partly digested milk. I move very slowly. I don't want to frighten him. I bring my face a tiny bit closer. Don't smile. Babies can sense fakes. The baby reaches out and pokes a finger gravely into the middle of my cheek. I release my hold with one hand, and carefully poke it back, touch my finger lightly on its cheek. The baby laughs. Just like that. And I smile quickly at him, glance up to see if anyone has seen.

No one is looking. Viv is sitting with her back to me. Carol has pulled up her sleeve and is showing everyone something on her wrist. I look back to the baby, who is reaching now for the stud in my ear.

'No way baby,' I say. 'No way, Joshua.'

Joshua lunges again for my ear and I take his wrist, bring it to my mouth and bite very softly into the white skin, make a low growling noise. Joshua laughs again.

When I glance back at the table, Carol is looking my way. She raises her eyebrows in a have-you-had-enough way. I shrug and smile as if to say we're fine. I wonder if Viv has told them.

I walk most days now. Sometimes twice. The bark is peeling from the gums in tattered strips and as I pass I allow names to attach to certain trees: old man, the twins, upside down pregnant woman. Sometimes Hil comes with me and I have to hurry to match her purposeful stride. 'Pretty buggerised up here, isn't it? Look at those blackberries in there; and that's holly coming up.' Kicking with the toes of her boots to dislodge the feral seedlings. When Hil comes we are always striking out on to new paths, elbowing aside bracken, getting twigs in our hair. 'What's down here? Where does this one go?' Or she wants to know about the history of the place, or the geological formation, or what is beyond.

'I reckon this must back on to the national park, Jess. Through there somewhere. You should get a map from Viv. You could probably get up into the mountains from here. Now that'd be a walk.'

Mostly I go alone. From the back of the nursing home a dirt path leads first around the oval, with its wooden stands and score-board, and then to the base of my hill. The first part is the steepest, up through a potholed paddock and then a cluster of pines. Bloody weeds, Hil says, but it is cool beneath them and the carpeted needles take away the sound of your footsteps. By the time I get to the top of the rise, my breath is hot and loud and fills my chest. I pause for a moment, watching for rabbits, and then set off along the ridge. Up here the path is wider, and sometimes there are fresh tyre tracks in the clay soil, perhaps from dirt bikes. I pass a blackened ring containing scorched tin cans and shards of brown glass and a little further on a rusted car exhaust protruding from the undergrowth.

The path drops and divides, one half disappearing to the right into an overgrown track, the other dipping towards a group of white-skinned gums. The grove, I call it, though it is not. It may

34

once have been a forest. The trees hold themselves like dancers and I walk among them powered by the deep combustion of breath. I do not think. Trees, birds, air, soil, self, light, in no particular order. The air cooling now, gathering scent and colour and sound, the looping cries of the currawongs. Cool in. Warm out. An exchange. And all around, the slow turbulence of the leaves.

At the top of the next rise, the forest drops away to scrub, and looking back I can see the shifting canopy and, above it, the clouds, which have been combed across the sky by some high wind. I squat and breathe. At my feet are small sticky seed pods, open now, and splayed into shapes of children's stars and flowers. The flesh that once contained the seeds is hard and nutty, the very wood peeled back by the force of expulsion.

One night I wake to the sounds of shouting down the corridor. A man's hoarse roar that stops as quickly as it starts. The swimmer. I lie for a long time afterwards in the dark, trying to push away the thoughts. How does a person drown? When I was nine I tried to do it in the bath. I wanted to see how it would feel. I stayed under until my cheeks were aching and there was a black beat at the base of my skull. 'That's not how you do it,' a girl at school said. 'You've got to open your mouth and let the water in. You have to breathe it.'

Irena is going home. Mr Ivanovich has organised wheelchair ramps and an invalid bathroom, and for their bedroom a new king-sized bed. Carers will come for an hour in the morning and two in the evening, to bathe and dress her or prepare her for bed. One evening a week, someone else will come and look after her so that Mr Ivanovich can go out and play cards with his friends, drink a little vodka. On Tuesdays, Irena tells me, the card-players will come to their house. 'Then I will serve them pelmeni and wear my new high shoes,' she says and snorts with laughter. But when she finishes, she is quiet, staring at the ceiling. For a moment she looks sad or frightened. I squeeze her shoulder lightly, and she turns towards me. 'Time you go too, Jess. I go home; you go home.' She nods emphatically.

After she has gone, the cleaner goes in. Five years of life. Behind the heater he finds a toy car, a blue pencil, a ring. When he has left, taking the last traces of Irena, I slip into the room and lie on her bed and stare at the ceiling. Above me, barely visible in the light, are the shapes of stars and planets, a slip of moon. I wonder how Irena will feel tonight in a big new bed, staring at an empty ceiling.

The next day, when I wake from my afternoon nap, her room is filled with voices. Viv's, the sandy doctor's, a woman, loud and insistent: 'This is just temporary, until we can find somewhere more suitable. He shouldn't be here.'

'He shouldn't be moved too soon,' says the doctor.

'And as I said over the phone, we'll have our own specialist working with him. He's flying in tomorrow.'

'Yes, well I don't want it disturbing the other residents,' says Viv.

When I walk past later the door is closed but I can hear the outline of voices. The woman's sharp peaks; a man's smoother curves. They are still there when I get back from my walk, and they keep talking, back and forth, until I fall asleep.

The following morning when I walk past the room on my way downstairs to breakfast, the door is half open. Peering in, I can see a woman's broad back slumped in one of Viv's moulded plastic chairs at the foot of the bed. A clump of brown wavy hair has come adrift from its clip. I try to look past her but from this angle most of the room is hidden and all I can make out is the end of the trolley; a bump that might be feet. When I come back, the door is closed again but, as I pass, it opens and a man steps into the corridor. He stops when he sees me and pulls the door shut behind him. He is tall and fine-boned, shoulders hunched slightly towards his chest, a thin grey face; over-large, wire-rimmed glasses behind which his eyes are pale and damp. He nods, still holding the handle, and I nod back and continue towards my room. As I reach my door he says, 'That's my son in there.'

I turn. He speaks quietly, not quite looking at me.

'I wonder…perhaps you might be able to pop in and say hello to him later? I'm taking my wife home for a couple of hours, she's done in. This business is killing her. She slept in here last night, in a sleeping bag, and she needs to freshen up before we go to the airport. We've got a specialist due in from Canada on a midday flight.'

'What's his name?'

'Orzasky. Dr Paul Orzasky.'

'I mean—your son.'

'Oh. I'm sorry. Hugh. His name's Hugh.'

Back in my room I lie on the bed and think about nothing. Shadows collect in the creases of Hil's vase, and the pigeons come and go without my looking. At eleven-fifteen Tina, I know her footsteps, comes along the corridor. She knocks lightly and when I don't answer, enters and puts something on my table. I keep my eyes shut as she goes into the next room. She is the only one who always knocks. She is in there a few minutes. I hear her voice. And then she leaves. I track her footsteps along the linoleum passage and down the stairs, and when I can no longer hear her, I get up. I take the envelope she has placed on the table and put it, without needing to check who it is from, in my shoulder bag. For later. Then I open the door, pulling it shut behind me.

The door to the next room is ajar. At first I just stand and listen, then I knock lightly, like Tina, and go in. The room looks smaller without Irena, empty. Gone are the pictures and framed photos, the woven rug that Steff hated, the brightly coloured bedspread. Against the whiteness of the sheets the walls look drab now, and the folded sleeping bag in the corner makes the room seem suddenly fleeting, provisional. The only sound is the boy's breath, a loose flapping like an unset sail. My bare feet are pale and wide against the red and grey fleck of the lino, and after a while I know that I don't want to look at him. I turn to leave and just then he begins to speak. Not speech. Not words. A man's low humming, made of half sounds and floating vowels. Scraps of torn paper. I stand there for what seems a long time among them. It is a young man's voice, richly sprung and pleasurable. At times a jumble of sounds, a child's crooned mouthings, and then building in cadence and rhythm, thickening almost to speech, fragments of tune, then falling away again. Once there is a sobbing sound that could as easily be laughter. And later, the same two notes played forwards then back, over and over. Almost music.

'He's a tenor,' says a voice at the door; the mother is standing there and I notice, before glancing away, that she has tears on her face. 'He was about to audition for the opera in Melbourne. They even rescheduled him, after the accident, in case he woke up in time for the second round.'

A scrap of brown and grey hair has fallen again from her clip and lies across the shoulder of her dress. I think, briefly, that she is one of those people who will always look messy. There is silence from the bed now, except for the corrugated breath, and from the corridor the sound of voices. The father's, low and deliberate, and another, quicker, lighter.

'We have found this amazing man,' the mother says to me now, words falling over themselves, 'we are putting our faith in this amazing, good man, this doctor. He is going to help our son.'

'He is going to do his best, Laura,' says the husband, behind us. And seeing me, 'Oh hello. Thanks for looking in.'

I am trying to leave but the doctor comes in, and there are introductions. 'Jess,' I say. 'I'm in the room next door. I just came in for a minute to see—'

He looks young for an imported specialist, perhaps in his forties, dressed in jeans and a striped blue-and-white T-shirt.

'A bloody clown, if you ask me,' Steff tells Tina later, as they pull the sheets from my bed and fling them into the laundry trolley.

'I asked Jess if she would keep Hugh company,' the father tells Laura, who squeezes my shoulder.

'Glad you could come,' says Paul Orzasky, pumping my hand. 'Excuse my outfit. I just got off a plane.'

'That's all right,' I say, edging towards the door.

'He has a beautiful face, doesn't he?' says Laura, looking towards the bed. I nod.

'Anyway,' I say, 'I should get going.'

'No, please. Stay for a bit,' she says, snatching quickly at my sleeve and then dropping it. She looks at her hand for a moment as if surprised, then lowers her voice a little. 'My daughter's on her way. I'll be all right then. Would you mind?'

'Laura?' Her husband looks across from the bed where he is standing with Dr Orzasky.

'It's okay,' I say.

Even so, when we cross to the bed I try at first not to look; to focus on the outline, not the face. When I do, I see that she is right. Her son is beautiful. He has his father's fine bones and his mother's wavy brown hair. His face is pale with bright spots of colour on each cheek, the nose dented from some old fall. There are no tubes, no scars, no feeding lines running into either nostril; he looks as if he is sleeping.

'I feed him,' says Laura. 'Myself.'

'I thought he wasn't conscious,' I say.

'Hugh.' She speaks to the boy. 'This is Jess. She's in the next-door room. She was in a coma like you. And now she's nearly ready to go home.' She turns to me. 'That's right, isn't it? That's what the nurse said.' She continues without waiting for an answer. 'His breathing's fine and he knows how to swallow,' she says. 'He lets me feed him. That's how I know he's going to be all right.'

'It's a good sign,' says Dr Orzasky, from where he stands at the foot of the bed, jotting pencilled notes into what looks like a school exercise book.

'We had to fight them, to get the feeding tube taken out,' says Laura. 'That's one of the reasons we got out of the last place. At least here they say we can give it a go. Not without a battle, I might add.'

'They're worried he'll choke,' the father explains quietly.

'Yes, and he hasn't.' She reaches out and runs her forefinger lightly across the sleeping man's concave cheek. 'As if I'm not able to feed my own child. What would they know?' She addresses the question to the son, and her husband on the other side of the bed gives a tiny shrug and says nothing.

Dr Orzasky has been watching from the base of the bed, and he moves up now to where Laura is standing. 'Laura, would you mind?' For a moment she looks confused, then she steps away quickly to allow him in.

The doctor looks down at the young man in the bed for what seems a long time. Then, reaching behind him for one of the plastic chairs, he sits and leans forwards to take Hugh's wrist. Then nothing. Just the boy's windy breath, and the doctor's. The father, Martin, is rubbing a finger rhythmically up and down the side of his nose, and Laura frowns at him from across the bed. He stops for a moment, then looks away from her and starts again. No one speaks, and after a while everyone's attention returns to Paul Orzasky. It takes me a while to realise that they are breathing now in unison, the doctor matching his patient. Long in. Long out. And then, on the exhalation, he begins to speak, softly, rhythmically, up against the boy's ear.

'Hugh,' says the doctor, 'I'm Paul – Orzasky – I've come a – long way to – see you. – I'm going – to try and – help get you – back on your – feet. – If that's what – you'd like. – I'm going to – examine you – now – as gently – as I can. – A couple of – these tests might – sting a little – but I won't – do anything – without letting – you know first. – Okay?'

I see Laura glance quickly at her husband. Paul Orzasky reaches and opens the case on the table near the bed head, and pulls out a slim black torch, talking all the while in his light voice with its long, sloping vowels. 'O-kay now.' He puts all the weight on the O-sound, kicking off with the K. 'I'm just going – to shine – this light – in your eyes – Hugh – just to check – what's going – on with them.'

He pulls back the eyelids, one by one. 'Okay, well there's – something happening – there, Hugh – glad to have – you with us.

'Does he move around much, Laura, Martin?'

'Not much,' says Martin.

'And talk? Does he say anything, make sounds, anything?'

'Sometimes,' says Laura, 'though he stops if he knows you're in the room.'

'He stops? Well that's a good sign. That's surely a good sign. What sort of sounds?'

'Oh, well, just sounds. Nothing really. Just…sounds.' She stops, uncertain, and for the first time since we have entered the room speaks to her husband. 'Martin?'

'A kind of singing,' says Martin. 'But without words.'

'Singing without words. Sounds nice. I'd like to hear that. Now I'm – just going to – tap your arms – and legs – Hugh – to test your – reflexes. – It may feel – a little – strange.'

Dr Orzasky pulls a small hammer-like instrument from his bag.

'He should never have moved to Melbourne,' says Laura suddenly. 'I knew something like this would happen. I knew it. I had a bad feeling.'

'Darling, you often have bad feelings, and quite often they don't amount to anything,' says Martin, quietly.

'How do you know? We should never have let him go.'

'Looks to me as if you didn't have much choice,' says Dr Orzasky conversationally, not looking up from the boy. 'How old did you say he was? Nineteen?'

She turns to me. 'He could have stayed here. He had an apartment of his own we'd bought him. Nothing big. It wasn't anything embarrassing. Just a little place over in Coogee. There's a good singing school here too. He knows that. He would have been in already. Wouldn't you?' She looks down at the young man on the bed, shaking her head, looks away as if she might start crying.

Martin clears his throat as if about to speak, and she turns, silencing him, face held, gaze blank. 'Not just me, Martin. Lucy says the same. That's his girlfriend,' she adds. 'Was. She's in Europe now on a scholarship. Beautiful voice. Lovely girl. God. You know. They could've—'

She pauses again, then accelerates. 'And instead he has to go off to Melbourne and live in some dump. Yes, Martin, it was a dump. And join some godawful rock band with those feral greenies. And get mixed up in all that. Where's the sense in that? I really would like to know if there's some sense to it all—'

She stops at last, teetering on some edge. Chewing her top lip. Dr Orzasky steps in.

'Okay, what we're doing here is trying to establish some base-line data to help us monitor Hugh's progress. Although to be honest I'm not all that interested in data, baseline or otherwise. I'm interested in results. And the sorts of results I tend to get don't seem to have much to do with what the data says. Still, it helps to have something down in writing for the cynics. And there's no shortage of them.'

Laura nods quickly and rhythmically, lips clamped.

'So Hugh, in the interests of science, I'm just going use a little needle to prick your legs and arms a few times. I'm just looking for what sort of response you've got.'

He reaches into his bag as he speaks, and draws out what looks like a normal sewing needle. 'Now, I won't do anything without telling you first. So get ready for a prick in your right leg— now.' He pecks the needle swiftly into Hugh's right calf. The leg seems to twitch, and Laura jumps. 'Okay buddy. That's great.' He repeats the procedure on the other leg, both arms, and stops to make more notes in his striped exercise book. There is a knock on the door. Tina enters. Seeing me, she raises her eyebrows a fraction, then speaks to Martin and Laura.

'Your daughter just rang. She said to tell you she'll be on a nine a.m. flight, and she'll be here by lunchtime tomorrow. She'll hire a car in Sydney.'

'Oh God, she shouldn't do that,' Laura turns to Martin, speaking quickly. 'She can use the Mazda, it's just sitting there, is she still on the phone?' She turns to Tina, who shakes her head. Martin moves around the bed and puts his arm around his wife's shoulders. 'It's all right, we'll sort it out.'

'But when will we? Chris's bloody phone's on the blink again, and she won't get a mobile. I wish she'd just get a mobile.' Her voice rises. 'Why is it that none of my children will speak to me?' Martin turns her to face him, puts his hands on her shoulders. 'Laura. Come here. Listen to me. We'll sort it out.'

She lets out a long, shuddering sigh and leans her head against his chest.

'Okay,' says Dr Orzasky. 'Why don't we all take a break? Go downstairs, grab a coffee. They do do coffee here I hope?'

'There's a machine,' says Martin, over Laura's head. 'I don't know that you'd call it coffee.'

'Lead me to it! Hugh, we'll take twenty minutes, then I'll come back and finish off these procedures. And we'll start the real work in the morning, when we're all fresh.'

In the corridor, I turn towards my room, and Martin steps quickly ahead and opens my door. 'Thank you,' he says.

'That's all right, I didn't do anything.' I shrug.

'Yes you did,' says Laura, recovered now, 'you gave us moral support.'

Dr Orzasky is already heading down the corridor. He stops and turns back. 'Come by tomorrow morning. After breakfast. That's when it gets really interesting.'

All through spring the ants have been finding their way inside. Sometimes at the end of the day I've found them in the empty shower cubicle, gathered around stray droplets of water, heads lowered like cattle to a trough. They drink with diligence. I lick my fingers before I turn on the shower and press them gently against each ant, one by one, just enough to hold them to my skin for a moment, then, leaning over the sink, I flick them out the window. It must be like falling from the moon. Sometimes I find the sink full of droplets; in each droplet a drowned ant. As if they have been engulfed by their own glistening reflections.

As if the water is drinking the ant.

The next morning I wait until I hear their voices moving along the corridor before I leave my room, heading towards them as if I might be on my way down to breakfast. Laura and Dr Orzasky are walking together, in conversation. Martin, behind them, the third point in the triangle. Laura quickens her pace when she sees me, opens her arms, kisses my cheek. 'Wonderful. You're here.'

I nod quickly, unable to think of anything to say.

The doctor grins at me.

'We're just up from breakfast,' says Martin.

'I'm late today,' I say. 'I didn't sleep very well.'

'Nor did we. Nor did we,' says Laura. 'The motel had fleas, I'm sure of it. I was more comfortable in my sleeping bag.'

'You slept nearly nine hours,' Martin tells her. Then to me, 'I persuaded her to sleep in a proper bed. Paul says it might be a long day.'

'All I got was a sore back,' continues Laura. 'Though the shower was nice.'

She reaches her hand out and places it lightly on my forearm. 'Will you come?'

Inside the room the boy is silent, a thin stream of spittle leaking down one cheek, which Laura wipes deftly with a tissue. His hands above the cotton bedspread are clenched slightly inwards from his wrists like claws or dried flowers. The chair near the head of the bed has been pushed back against the wall, and Dr Orzasky pulls it forwards again, scraping it over the lino, to sit next to Hugh's head. He says nothing at first, again aligning his breathing with the boy's, then speaks on the out breath.

'Hello Hugh – this is Paul – Orzasky – again – I'm here with – your father – and your – mother and – a new friend – of yours – called Jess – who is – very – pretty.'

He glances at me quickly, winks, and continues, while I look at the woven bedspread and away from Laura's smile.

'In a – moment – I am – going to – touch you – gently – on your arm. – Now you – can feel – the pressure – of my hand. – I am – pressing – in time – with your – breathing. – Wherever – you are – right now – whatever's – happening – in your world – I want you – to just go – with it – to feel – how it feels – and don't – be afraid – I'm here – with you.'

In the silence that follows, Martin examines his fingers, and Laura keeps her gaze fixed on her son. Dr Orzasky goes back to his breathing. And for several minutes there is just the rise and fall of breath. Slow in. Slow out. It is a comforting, familiar sound, and soon I notice that my breathing falls in with theirs, my shoulders loosen. And then Hugh coughs. At first I think it is the doctor clearing his throat. We all glance quickly towards him. But he has leaned in closer, looking intently at the young man's face, frowning in concentration.

'Oh, I heard that,' he says approvingly. 'I know what you mean.' And then he too coughs. A deeper, fleshier sound. He waits half a minute and coughs again. In the silence of the room Laura and Martin exchange glances. Dr Orzasky closes his eyes and from outside a magpie's cry bubbles up and up and I remember suddenly sitting in a classroom as a child, the gouged wooden desks and the scrape of pencils on paper; outside, blue sky and bitumen and beyond that the oval, and somewhere beyond that Hil's house and knowing that she will be there at three to get me.

There is another cough, and another, longer, and then a third that stretches into a rasping sound and gagging. Laura starts, and reaches towards the boy's head, as if to raise it. The doctor places his free hand on her forearm and holds it until she looks at him. He shakes his head a little then clears his throat loudly, a full, phlegmy vowel sound. 'Ah, that's better,' he says, expansively. 'It's good to clear the throat. Isn't it Hugh?' And he does it again, louder still. The boy lies still. From across the bed, Martin raises his eyebrows slightly at Laura. We have all stepped back except the doctor, who is once more looking intently at Hugh; bent, almost hunched, towards him, matching him again breath for breath.

The room seems hot and heavy with small irrelevant sounds, the vacuum cleaner from downstairs, the *b-b-b* as Martin, gazing now at the ceiling, forces tiny bubbles of air through his pursed lips, like a fish. I wonder if I should turn on the ceiling fan, or maybe just leave. Laura clears her throat as if to speak. And this time Paul Orzasky makes a sudden swift chopping motion with his hand in front of her, shakes his head and mouths the word 'no'.

Laura's shoulders stiffen. She takes a breath, closes her mouth and turns away, and suddenly from the bed comes a low growling sound.

'Yeaaah,' sighs Paul Orzasky, 'that's great.' Without looking away from the bed he reaches his hand towards Laura again and takes her wrist, patting it softly, rhythmically with his thumb, as if to both soothe and restrain.

'Yeah,' he says again, full voiced now, and then close to the boy's ear, rasping, almost growling himself, 'it's good to clear it out, isn't it? Good to get it out.'

The boy growls again, a long, stuck sound, like a car revving in neutral, that dies with his breath. And then the arm closest to Dr Orzasky, his left arm, lying bent across his chest, starts to twitch. The doctor lets go of Laura's wrist and takes Hugh's arm lightly with both his hands, one above, one below the elbow. At first he holds the arm loosely, just following its motion.

'Yes, yes,' he says to the boy, 'that's a wonderful movement.' And then gradually he begins to enlarge on the movement, or perhaps the movements just increase. It is hard to tell. It goes on for another minute or two, the arm opening a little wider each time, until the doctor has to move his chair back and take his hands away to avoid being hit.

'That's a big, open movement,' he says, sounding impressed. 'That feels fantastic.' He pauses, then adds deliberately, 'That feels fan-fuckin'-tastic.' Almost immediately the other arm starts to twitch, then jerk, away from the boy's chest. The movement increases rapidly, in staccato bursts, guided by Dr Orzasky, until it is matching that of the other arm, both open, stretched forwards and out, like a child. And there they seem to get stuck, still jerking rhythmically, but rigid, neither opening nor closing. Hugh is sweating, tiny raised bubbles across his forehead. And I am momentarily aware that all of us are giving off odour. It hangs above and between us, a clumped human smell of breath and perspiration and focus.

'Whoa there. Hey buddy I'll just give you a hand. Okay Hugh, I'm with you.' The doctor stands and turns to face the boy, his back to Laura, and reaching across Hugh's body takes his wrists in his hands. He stands like that for a few seconds and then gently but firmly begins to press the outsides of the boy's forearms, as if to fold them back on to his chest. For a moment the boy's arms appear to relax, as if about to subside towards each other, but then they tense again, pressing back against the doctor.

The two men seem to stay locked there against each other, exerting an equal, even force, until suddenly the boy's mouth moves. A quick spasm. He grimaces, lips pulled back, the blood vessels beginning to stand out on his arms and temples. Even now, weeks after the accident, the skin of his arms is a soft brown, the muscles clearly defined. Laura takes a step forward, hesitates, glances at the doctor, her husband, her son, and speaks.

'Is this necessary? I really don't see—' she begins, ignoring Paul Orzasky, who frowns, and opens his mouth as if to remonstrate. Perhaps he does. At the same moment Hugh lifts his face now towards the ceiling, arches his neck, opens his mouth and lets out a cry so loud it startles the pigeons on Viv's elm, a band of sound so clear and wide it might have come from a trumpet, a horn, a conch. Steadily he opens his arms, pushing Dr Orzasky's apart and finally away, all the time holding that long, pure note that keeps on and on, fading at last with the breath, only to be followed by another, and another.

*

Afterwards I go downstairs. In the garden, a young woman sits on a wooden bench with a pram in front of her, the child propped and plump. The woman pulls the pram close and then pushes it out to arm's length, the baby laughing in hiccoughs of delight as it comes close again. 'Bah,' says the woman, and the pram goes back. 'Bah, bah,' a breath in his face each time they are near.

'Bah,' says the baby, and then, 'ba ba.'

The woman's face pulls to an expression of delight. She claps her hands. 'That's right,' she says, pointing at his chest, 'Bubba. Bubba.'

'Bubba,' says the child again, beaming, and claps his hands.

'Bubba. That's right. You're the bubba. My beautiful, clever Bubba.'

To reach the gate I have to walk past them and, as I approach, the woman looks up for a moment and includes me in her smile. 'Bubba,' she says again, as I pass.

Anna comes by unexpectedly the next afternoon, while I am napping. She taps lightly at the door and enters without waiting for an answer. 'Hello Jess, how are you? The doctor tells me you're doing well.'

'That's nice of him,' I say, raising myself only slightly in the bed. 'I'm not feeling very well.' It's true. My lower back aches. My head feels spongy, unreceptive.

'Why do you think that is?' she asks, pulling the chair by my bed around so that she is facing me.

'I don't know.' I shrug and hunch further down into the bedding. 'I just feel sick. I think I might be getting some sort of flu again.'

'It's that time of year.' She nods. 'A few of my clients are feeling under the weather. Have you sorted out what you're going to do when you leave here?'

'No, not yet. I—'

'So, you've got some decisions to make, then.'

'I just need to be really well before I—'

'Jess, there are always plenty of viruses around. That's life. That's what your GP's for.'

'I just don't think I'm quite well enough.'

'It's time to go home, Jess.'

She says it quite gently, not taking her eyes from mine.

'You have a child to look after.'

II

A long time ago, at a dinner party in a house with harbour views, I found myself sitting next to a man who turned out to be a psychiatrist. It was the first formal dinner party I had been to, the men in suits, the women, even me, in expensive dresses and the table set with three knives, one for fish. The man I had come with, who I would shortly marry, was seated on the other side of the table, at the far end. From time to time he would glance up and smile quickly and reassuringly, but from where I was sitting I could barely even hear his voice above the others. I did not know which wine glass to use. I did not know what to drink. The host, who was tall and tanned and looked as if he played tennis, offered me a selection of whites, and I could feel my mouth open and close two or three times, fishlike, before the man beside me, who was balding with a reddish face, suggested the Chablis. And I said 'Righto' and reached for a glass, which turned out of course to be the wrong one. The psychiatrist was there because he was married to a paediatric anaesthetist, like half the people at the table I supposed—like me, almost—and although he looked, I thought, puffy and old, I realised after a while that he probably felt as out of place as I did and started to like him a little.

He was a good listener. He asked me about my job, so I told him about the business my friend Emma had set up (where I had met Michael) publishing medical books for the non-medical public, and about working there as a book editor, at least for now. He said that he was a great reader but tried to avoid medical books, and I said so did I and we laughed and talked for a while about novels and then the role of fiction, which he said was to remind people of things they did not know they had forgotten.

Then the conversation turned inevitably back to anaesthesia. It was the host's birthday so there was a speech and doubtless a lot of hospital jokes, and while the cake was being cut the psychiatrist said that occasionally his wife referred a patient on to him; if they had not coped well with the general anaesthetic, for example, or had come back to her later as they sometimes did, complaining of anxiety or sleeplessness.

Everyone had started to stand now, pushing back their chairs, heading to the balcony for champagne and cigarettes. The psychiatrist put his hands on the table as if to push himself up, then sank back again.

'You know,' he said, 'you could take any of the people in this room and, if they were suitable subjects, with a very simple procedure you could take them back so they could recall with remarkable clarity events that they had no idea they still remembered.

'Take Brian over there,' he said, nodding towards the host. 'If he were a good subject, I could guide him back to his tenth birthday, or his eighth or his fifth.'

I wanted to ask him what made a good subject but, seeing Michael moving towards us, I laughed and said I wasn't sure that I would want to remember any of my birthdays. Then we all walked out on to the balcony, Michael cupped his warm palm around the nape of my neck, and the psychiatrist dipped his head and wandered off, he said, to locate his wife.

I rang three weeks later and after reminding him of our conversation, asked if I could come and see him. He had a medium-sized room in a largish terrace in Potts Point. From his front window, peering between the slats of the wooden venetians, I could make out the grey bulk of the naval frigates in the harbour and the skeletal tip of the old finger wharf. The psychiatrist asked how he could help me and then directed me to a corduroy armchair opposite him. After explaining that we would start with a relaxation exercise, he asked me to close my eyes. It was all very simple and less fraught than I had expected. He was friendly but unobtrusive; his voice, which at the party had seemed almost wheezy, was in this room calm and solid.

At the end, he counted backwards from five, like in the movies. When I opened my eyes all I could see was dust revolving slowly in the slatted afternoon light.

'How was that?' he asked.

I told him it had been, as he had indicated, remarkably straightforward: like watching a film I had seen before, but so long ago I had forgotten the plot. 'Enthralling but unsurprising,' I said and started to cry.

The psychiatrist said I was a good subject for hypnosis and

that perhaps I might want to come back and talk to him again. I said I would think about it, but in the end I didn't. It was just the shock, I told myself later, of having found a whole day curled inside me, gleaming and wet like a child.

III

I set out across the oval, today filled with school children, past the scoreboard, through the gap in the wire fence and up the incline towards the pine trees.

'I'm going to go for a bushwalk,' I told Anna, that last time I saw her, before I left the nursing home for good. 'Just part of the way up the mountain. It'll only take a couple of days.'

'Jess, did you hear what I said?'

'Yes.'

It is hard walking with the pack on my back. Inside is a two-man tent—'two-person; can't be sexist,' said the guy at the camping shop, hoping to be funny—a small cooker, one change of clothes, enough food for two days I hope; a map, a torch. Even not quite full, it digs into my hips and drags at my shoulders. I stop at the ridge, readjust my shoulder straps, swig from my water bottle. When I reach the path at the top, I pause again and look down to my left towards the grove of trees where I usually walk.

I think about taking off my pack and hurrying down to—to do what? Touch them. Say goodbye. Instead I pull out the map from my pouch and take the narrower path veering to the right that leads up into the mountains. I plan as I walk, matching my thoughts with the rhythm of my boots. Straight on for a couple of kilometres, then hook on to the road for a bit, and then back into the bush and the main track up the mountain. The air is cool and astringent, twisting through the tops of the eucalypts. Try for maybe twenty kilometres today, maybe a little less. Make sure I've got plenty of time to set up the tent, light a fire, cook some soup before dark. My stomach tightens a little at the thought of the dark, so I think about the torch I bought yesterday and the new set of batteries, and of the women's self-defence course I never finished and Hil trying to teach me karate on Bondi Beach, and of the concrete and iron balustrade above the middle of the beach where my husband and I used to watch dolphins riding the waves with the surfers.

I trip on a tree root and stagger, the backpack tipping me abruptly off balance. I grab a low branch for support, then pull myself up and start to take the pack off, my heart jittery with adrenaline, my fingers shaking on the clip. For the first time in months I feel a rush of craving for a cigarette. I am only a kilometre or so from the nursing home, but it feels further. Irrevocable. I breathe deeply and try to feel inside for that calm, cocooned self, the self I have grown to trust. An anxious wind skitters through the canopy, bending the branches back upon themselves, sending a twig scraping through the foliage to my feet.

Viv has given me two apples from her garden at home. I pull one from the side pocket of the pack, and crouch on a low lichen-splattered rock to eat it. 'I hope you know what you're doing,' she said. Not smiling. 'I don't want to see you back here.' The flesh is tart and sweet. I put the core in my bag, thinking of Hil, feeling better. The map shows a campsite about six hours' walk away, I estimate, taking it slowly up the mountain track. That might do.

'Have you thought,' said Anna, 'about what you will do when you leave here?'

'Not really. I might stay with my aunt, Hil.'

'What about your husband?'

'I don't know.'

The map is in the front pocket of the backpack, along with a small packet of tissues I bought at the chemist and some barley sugars for energy. The bloke at the camping shop gave me the map. 'You won't need it,' he said, when I asked. 'Just follow the path.' But I said no, I liked to know where I was going.

'Fair enough,' he said. 'Cheers. On the house.'

I wanted to buy a drink flask too, but I didn't want him to think I expected that for free. And it seemed a good time to leave, our encounter rounded with a gift and cheers. I'd get bottled water from the milk bar. Cheaper.

'You travelling alone?' he asked as I shrugged the pack over my shoulders.

'No.'

When I think of my husband I think of a block, a square, four straight lines, and all my life streaming towards it and then stopping. Even now, even from this distance, if I try to bring it close, to look at it, my mind veers away, becomes vague, unfocused, and I find nothing. I feel nothing.

'Tell me how that is in your body,' said Anna.

'How what is?'

'Nothing.'

'What?'

'Tell me how it is to feel nothing.'

'That's the whole point,' I said, irritated. 'I don't feel anything. I feel nothing. It's like a black box.'

'Can you describe the box?' she said.

Silence.

'How big is it?'

'I don't know.' I held my hands up in front of my chest, where the box resides, made a square from my thumbs and forefingers.

'What is it made from? How does it feel?'

'Rock. Stone. Not shiny. I don't know. Something heavy. It feels heavy.'

We are in drought. Radio bulletins about stock losses, half-empty reservoirs, water restrictions. You don't notice it up here, where the bush holds its blues and greens in taut, tarpaulin spearheads and sun-resistant spikes. But in the suburbs you can sense the strain in the wheaten lawns, the early morning hosing; even the birch leaves in Viv's garden curling brown at the edges.

'This black box,' said Anna, 'this heavy black box in your chest; if it could speak, if it could tell me something or ask me something, what would it say?'

I looked away, down at the floor. Anna said nothing. We were sitting cross-legged on cushions, facing each other, about two metres apart in the private counselling room downstairs. The carpet was beige with darker grey smudges. I glanced back at her, then down again.

'Can you tell me what might it say?' she asked again, in a quiet voice. 'What does it need?'

'It doesn't need anything,' I said quickly, surprising myself at the force of my voice. I knew, even as I spoke, that I'd given something away, unprepared, that she knew more about me than I had intended.

I waited for her to say something, but she was silent. After a couple of moments, still looking down, I said, 'It would ask for help.'

When I looked up she nodded slowly.

'But?' she said.

'But what?'

'It would say, help me, but what?'

'I don't know what you mean.'

'Help me, but keep away? Is that what it would say?'

I looked down, then up again into her eyes.

'Yes. That is what it would say.'

When I lie awake in the early hours of the morning, sometimes, if I can let it, if I don't clench against it, everything starts to move. A rolling, swirling motion. I think of the inside of storm clouds, air and water billowing incessantly, changing shape. If I am relaxed enough, close enough to sleep, I let myself go with it and then I too am just movement, a building up and breaking down, drifting and recompiling. In the moments that I am in it, the sensation is exquisite, a delicate rushing, a dismantling. Occasionally I stay with it and am adrift in bliss. Normally, though, what happens is a sort of vertigo or motion sickness. The self starts to reassert itself, a shadow at the edges, a grey wash that works to separate me from other, to define me. And with this comes constriction, contraction. My body tenses, my mind makes shapes. I hold myself still.

'Try saying it,' she said.

'Saying what?'

'Help me. But keep away.'

'Now?'

'That's right. Help me, but keep away. Try it out.'

I looked away, towards the door, outside which I could hear the shuffle-drag of someone moving along the corridor behind a walking frame. It must be nearly time. I glanced back across Anna's shoulders to the small round clock she kept on the shelf above her desk. Nearly. I was self-conscious, my body fidgety, ungainly.

'Can we leave it until next time?'

'Now would be better,' she said matter-of-factly. 'Now is when you have the energy.'

'Out loud? Does it have to be out loud?'

She smiled, nodded.

'What am I saying again? What do I have to say?'

'You could try saying, help me.'

'And I have to look at you?'

'Yes.'

Quickly, to get it over with, I said it. 'Help me.' A small fish flip-flopping on the table.

68

'Good. Say it again.'

'Help me.' A bit louder this time. 'Help me.' I said it a couple more times. But I gave them to her as if they were not my words, as if someone else had left them here and I was merely passing them on; someone I felt a bit ashamed for, and sad.

She nodded. 'Now try saying keep away.'

'Keep away.' I said it instantly. I tried to keep it neutral, even, but it filled my throat, my mouth, voice. We both felt it.

'Well done,' she said. Then, after a pause, 'I think there is more force in the second one.'

'Me too.'

For the first time I smiled. I met her look. She was smiling too.

The map shows the start of the trail marked by a small butterfly shape, which I decide must be a gate. Now that I am through the undergrowth, the other side of my hill ends disconcertingly in the backs of houses, fences of wood marking off houses of brick. I find myself in a cul de sac, a keyhole-shaped street of about ten allotments on each side, ending in a round turning circle, which is where I enter, through a track between houses. The bitumen is shiny black and two of the homes are still under construction. I doubt that I'll find it on the map. But when I look it is here, among the dotted lines marking out other unfinished courts and crescents and an avenue or two. They are big houses, double-storey, with balconies and gables and two-car garages. One or two have bikes leaning up outside, or bright plastic scooters. One has a toddler pool sitting on the yellow lawn, but no water.

As I approach this house, walking along the road, I notice

a cattle dog lying on its side in the driveway. I glance at it quickly, then look away, not wanting to aggravate it. I cannot remember whether you are meant to lower your eyes or outstare them. He looks relaxed, but it is hard to tell with heelers; they can be territorial, and bored. As I walk away past the house I can feel the spot on the back of my exposed calf where a dog might bite, where that dog might bite. It is so vivid I can almost feel my right leg throbbing. I am completely absorbed in the sensation, though dimly aware that I should shift my attention, move my mind away, when I hear a small sound behind me and the dog bites. It does not bite hard. The skin is not broken and it does not hurt. It is almost a relief, corresponding so exactly to my expectation.

I stop and turn. The dog is standing a few paces away looking at me more in puzzlement than anything else, alert but not aggressive. We meet eyes for a moment, each implicated. 'Go on now,' I say quietly, and keep walking without thinking or looking back.

At the end of this street is a slightly larger one, along which I travel for a few metres before turning on to another smaller, keyhole street, which leads me back, as abruptly as I emerged, on to a dirt track and into bushland. I walk on for maybe half a kilometre until the houses disappear, and am about to pull out the map again when I see ahead of me a rusted green metal sign and beyond it, further into the trees, a metal gate.

It is odd to find myself missing it now, the nursing home, my small room, Tina, Maud. One night a couple of weeks after I came to, I woke to the smell of cigarette smoke. It was a strange smell, no longer appealing, but an alliance even so. I lay for a while, wondering about the smoker, and then I shuffled to my window and quietly opened it. Through the darkness I could make out a darker shape on the bench outside the kitchen, and a small orange point that flared and subsided with each breath. After a while a voice from below said, 'Sorry love, am I keeping you awake?' And I said, no, I wasn't much of a sleeper anyway.

'Join the club,' said the voice. 'Coming down?'

It took me a while to navigate the stairs, feeling foolish, hoping the voice and the dark shape would not disappear. Maud introduced herself, although we had seen each other around the home already. She walked with a wooden stick, which I had heard Viv trying to persuade her to exchange for an aluminium one with a rubber hand grip and four prongs at the bottom for stability.

'Too late for that,' Maud had said.

Now we shook hands, hers fleshy and very soft.

'You look better than you did,' she said, and I nodded and asked her how long she had been there and she said 'too bloody long' and laughed her big wheezy laugh, and for the first time since arriving, just for a moment, I felt happy. After that we would meet downstairs every now and again; the midnight club, Maud called it, although normally it was later, three or four, and often we did not talk.

When we saw each other in the daytime, she would nod or wink, but that was generally all, although one day she walked across the dining room and hugged me, just like that, with her big bread-maker's arms, and I felt enveloped and shocked and replete.

I stop at the gate and pull out the map again. The trail I intend to follow zig-zags through whorls of crimson contours and across the hospital green of the national park. At the top edge of the map, a few kilometres to the north (in acid yellow) is domesticity: black train line, red highway, cream teas. Here where I am about to go is wilderness. Each existing side by side, almost merging at times, but each unknown, unknowable to the other.

When I look up a bike rider is approaching down the path. He has his head down low and is making a good speed, the back of the bike sliding once as he swerves to avoid something on the road. In his glossy synthetics and plastic pointed helmet, he looks for a moment constructed, electronic, like a remote-control toy. He pulls to a stop in front of me, heat dancing around him, face shiny with sweat. So full of movement, even at a standstill, that he feels to be closer to me than he is, and I step back.

'Sorry,' he says; he is breathing deeply and evenly, not puffed, simply absorbed, all of him, in the process of motion.

I stand back while he dismounts and hurdles the gate before reaching back to lift the bike across. 'You walking?' he asks, and when I nod, he says, 'Take you a while. It's uphill.'

I nod again. There is an opening in the fence a few metres away and I walk around, rather than try to mount the fence, grace-less with my pack.

As he rides off, he calls behind him: 'Not much of a trail. Nothing to see.' But I am not here to see. And so I raise my hand and keep walking. Almost immediately, the town, or the idea of town, drops away.

Everything is burnt. Up here the trees are black twigs, pushed into the ground by a child, brittle scarecrow arms raised to the sky. Abrupt, irrevocable. A shape passes above me and looking up I see a small hawk, quite low, gliding and looking. There are not many places to hide. The soil must be rich now, dusted still with pale ash, nutrients from the bodies of trees and small animals that lived in the hollows.

The fires were a year ago. I remember vaguely hearing about them in the news, fires in the national park. But there are always fires, one year or another. And the park held no meaning for me then, or the trail that I am now walking. Perhaps these weren't the fires they were talking about. Perhaps those ones were higher up, closer to homes. Perhaps this fire was not even noted or reported on.

The road disappears behind me as I round the first bend, and continues ahead in a shallow, steady incline. As I walk, my hip bones rub through my skin against the strap of the pack. I am losing my plumpness. And for all the years of hoping for this lessening, I now feel less than, unsatisfactory. After about ten minutes I stop and take off my pack, sit down on the edge of the road. For a moment all I can hear is myself, my breath, already pushing a little at my chest, and my heart.

'Jess, wake up.' It is a whisper, just a whisper, and I cannot tell who is speaking.

I wonder now about the specialist from town. It annoys me, the way he talked about my coma. 'Your coma,' he said. My coma: as if I were responsible for it, as if it belonged to me, rather than the other way around. As if, too, there were a clear line between what was me and what was it: my coma; as if we were separate.

'Tell me about your coma,' said the specialist's colleague (he was fiftyish and handsome, with a complacent, boyish face and dry patches at the corners of his mouth where he had forgotten to moisturise); and then, when I continued to stare at him, unresponsive, he tried a different approach. 'Let me recast the question,' he said. 'How, when you woke up, did you know that you were awake?' He looked pleased with himself.

'I was awake because I wasn't asleep,' I said evenly, before Hil arrived and made them leave.

We both knew it was not an answer; I could see him writing on his clipboard as he walked to the door, but what was I supposed to say? A coma has an inside and an outside, and whichever side you find yourself on, even fleetingly, you cannot grasp the other? I was awake because I was on the outside of the coma and I couldn't get

74

back. Even if I'd wanted to. Even though I'd wanted to.

I could hardly tell him that. He would have been delighted.

Besides which, it was only partly true. A better question might have been, what did my coma feel like, or how did I feel about my coma. And even then I could not have told him. It changes all the time. But when I think about my coma now, what comes to me, or what rises in me, or around me, is a feeling that I cannot name, which might be grief or might be joy, or fullness, or emptiness. I can taste it now, pooled in the back of my throat. An exquisite tender ache. Everything else is the casing. Muscle, rock, shell. Everything else is just layers.

That is how I feel about my coma.

Ten-twenty-five and already everything feels wrong: the blackened trees; my legs, pasty where they protrude from the shorts, hairs half-grown and spiky, calves already pink despite the sun block. Thin-skinned, Michael said, a blusher. As a child, an adolescent, the mottled tide rising up my neck, chin, cheeks, prickling my scalp. Even the tiniest of slights. Even a thought. And everyone then able to see for themselves. In winter I prefer high-necked jumpers. And even in summer, even in this heat, I like to be covered. I hide my chest and the base of my throat. My heart settles gradually, and with it my breathing. I open my water bottle and swallow.

You can turn back: I say the words so I can hear them in my head. I can turn back. I can catch a cab back to the station. And from there a train. In two hours I can be home. (But where is home?) I can ring Hil. She will meet me at Central. I can take it from there, make a plan; we can talk it through, think it over, I can sleep on it. Whatever. I squat a little way from the path and watch the piss spurt, feel the strain in my thighs, the new grass sharp against my buttocks. Black trees and thin blue sky. I pull the pack on and continue.

Underneath the stick trees the black ground is striped with brilliant green, blades and locks and tresses of green, grasses so fine you could thread them through a needle, and wider-leaved, saw-edged tufts, like pineapple tops. Once you get over the black, the green is everywhere, sprouting in foolish, furious clumps from the branches and even the trunks of the charcoaled trees. Occasionally among them the trunk of an angophora bursts bright orange or salmon pink from its blackened casing. Once your eye is in, all you see is colour.

Now that I have made my decision I enter for a while a dreamy hollow of walking, a passage of time in which I am protected from the flickering doubts that have been with me since leaving the nursing home. The path is pink and sandy and has its own momentum, the black and green of the trees alternating beside me. A landscape abbreviated, comforting even, in its starkness: the sense that the worst has already happened, and I am still here.

It is not, I am aware, real bushwalking. I have a map but no compass. And although the map shows that I must now be a considerable distance from any houses, some kilometres into the national park, I am on a fire trail. There is no chance of getting lost. Nor is there any chance of stumbling across an unexpected waterfall or swimming hole—as I might have, if I had plotted my own course. Once, in the distance, I see what might be a small snake uncurl itself from the side of the road and slip into the bushes as I approach, but it disappears before I reach it, and might have been a lizard.

The road is surprisingly uneven. Despite the evidence of the map, I had imagined a straight, steady incline. Instead, it curves this way and that, though more, it seems, to the left. To the west, or what I imagine to be west; I can no longer tell. Either way, for the most part the land is higher to my left. The road is steep in parts and rippled, with potholes and fissures where the earth, yellower as I get higher, has cracked open or been washed away. After heavy rain it is almost impassable, the guy in the mountain shop said. A slippery torrent, clutching as it passes at sand and clay and small stones.

Now and again I stumble, the impact travelling up my leg to the small of my back. Careful. It is smoother on the other side of the road, but I follow the inside of the curve, clinging mainly to the left. I tell myself that it will even out, and that this way I have to cover less distance. But in truth, I cling to the left because I am afraid of being hit by a bike. Any moment, I keep thinking, a group of riders, three, maybe more, could come sliding around one of these corners. They wouldn't be expecting me, or looking. It is not logical, I know; as my husband would point out, I am better off on the outside of the curve, where I can be seen, and see. But I stick to the inside, where I feel safer. And my husband is not here.

As I walk, placing my feet carefully so as not to twist my ankle on a loose rock or another tree root, I think about the riders. In the end I can no longer tell whether I want them to come or not. In one version they are a cheerful force, raising their hands as they pass, perhaps even stopping briefly to tell me about conditions further up the path and wish me well. In another, they are simply careless—skidding around a corner too fast and striking me or at least showering me with dust. In the third—Stop.

The land to my left is raised, a shallow clay embankment, too familiar already, embedded with repetitive truncated concerns—bikers and snakes and other possibilities. I look to my right. A cluster of angophoras, five of them together. Through the trees, the land falls away a little and I can make out a ridge, or fragments of ridge, that seems to run parallel to the path. It does not look far, though it is hard to get a sense of perspective from here. Beyond the containing green of the angophoras the landscape appears in patches mainly as a khaki monotone with little in the way of gradient or features, the eye lulled or deadened by the sameness. I look at my watch. Eleven. Two hours' walking behind me. Lunch in an hour. In the pocket of my shorts is a fruit and nut bar, which I open without stopping, pushing the plastic wrapper carefully back into my pocket. It is sweet and chewy, not the sort of food I like, but satisfactory for now, the teeth bracing themselves against the stickiness of the sugar.

'Jess,' says Anna, quiet, persistent, 'what about your husband?'

I am thinking again about the nursing home. From the window of my room, if you leant out a little you could see, below, the kitchen door and beside it the old wooden bench where I used to sit in the dark with Maud while she smoked her sneaky fags. Sometimes in the daytime Tina and Steff sat there when they had a break. Steff with her head tilted back against the wall, blue-trousered legs straight out in front of her, Tina, on the occasion that now comes to mind, inclining forward over the woollen rug she was crocheting for her baby niece.

She is big, Steff, bigger than Hil or me, set on a solid steel frame. Not fat, or if she is it all seems useful or necessary. She has

thick dark hair which she pulls back in a ponytail with those coloured hair bands you buy from the chemist in lots of twelve or six,
and which disappear, in my experience, almost immediately you
have opened the packet. She would have been the sort of girl I
avoided at school, uninterested in showy displays (boys, makeup,
fallings in and out), unsmiling except within her coterie. When
Steff was in the same room as me I felt that I was back at school and
that I was on the outer.

I could not make out what they were saying, on this day,
except for the occasional lilt of Tina's clear voice and, once, a deep
sharp burst of laughter from Steff. It is odd to think of them as
friends and perhaps they are not, away from the home, but they sat
together for quite a while and each time I looked out they were still
caught up in conversation. Once when one of Tina's balls of wool
rolled from her knees on to the gravel, Steff leapt forward, surprisingly graceful, and dusted it off before handing it back. Almost
gallant. After a while they both stood up and Tina put away her
wool, then they disappeared inside. When they reappeared each
was pushing a wheelchair, and after a moment Steff went inside for
another, then another, until there they were: four old ladies lined up
on the asphalt, their backs to the sun.

After a while Steff disappeared inside again and Tina sat
down on the bench. When she saw me coming, she waved and asked
if I would mind waiting with the ladies for a while. From the plastic
container on the bench beside her she brought out hand-cream,
scissors, tissue paper and a nail file. 'Here you go,' she said. 'Make
yourself useful.'

I started with Mrs McClintock. The skin that stretched over
her bones was like baking paper, translucent, decorated with

brownish circles and deep blue, almost black, veins. Her nails were long and thick, horn-like. 'Here, Eileen, can I give you a bit of a manicure?' The thumbnail was the thickest, ridged and yellowish over the small shrunken digit; the tiny delicate bones beneath encased in skin, articulated by stringy bands of tendon or ligament that I could feel around each joint.

'Careful dear, careful. Don't take my fingers off with those scissors.'

'I won't Eileen, I promise. I didn't mean to frighten you.'

'Not so much frightened, dear, as watchful.'

Even so her hand flinched each time the scissors bit into the nail, and I had to hold her fingers quite firmly between mine—'nearly there'—to get it done. She had no children, although a nephew came every few weeks and wheeled her along the footpath, sometimes around the block. 'I don't know why he does it,' she once said tartly. 'It jolts me terribly, rushing along at that pace.' Although whenever I watched he always seemed to be moving carefully and not fast, stopping every few paces to lean forwards to hear what she was saying. He must have come from work, in his lunch hour, as he always wore a suit. Lawyer maybe, except there were not too many lawyers around here, or not the suit-wearing type. Perhaps he was an accountant, or a manager, a person who managed things. He was tall and big-limbed with wide shoulders and neat brown hair. He would be a safe person, I thought, careful, considerate. The way he lowered his head towards her. I wondered if he had a wife and kids.

After an hour or so Steff came out again to wheel them into the dining room for lunch. I was just finishing off and I glanced at her and she looked straight past me, as she always did, and I looked away. I wondered if anyone else noticed, Tina or Viv or any of the other staff. I mentioned it once to Tina, that Steff didn't like me, but Tina shrugged and said not to worry about Steff, she was just like that.

When I think of my husband, it is in segments. The cropped beard, the full lips, the long thin fingers. In my mind, each is separate. And with each image comes a grey band of feeling. A pressure, distaste. I try to pull him together, force him together, and the grey feeling tightens and darkens, and I stop. My husband is a thick, dark feeling in my stomach. Aubergine. Bruised.

'He seems like a nice chap,' said Hil the first time I brought him home to the little wooden house where I was living with her again.

I laughed and said, 'Yes; yes he is a nice chap.' Chap: a very Hil word.

That night we walked down to the beach, the three of us, and ate mussels in sweet tomato sauce in one of the open air cafes that Hil usually mocked. Michael and I drank red, and Hil, as always, apple juice. Afterwards we all walked down on to the broad white beach and then along the sea path that followed the cliff to Bronte. At the top of the stone steps the path spreads out into an uneven rocky overhang that flows towards the ocean and then stops. We walked to the edge, all of us, and lowered ourselves on to our bellies on the still-warm rocks; looking straight down into the listing blue darkness and the rims of white foam far below, until after a minute I felt dizzy and turned, half crawling, back towards the path. Michael helped me up, supporting my elbow, and I felt awkward and pleased but did not catch his eye, nor Hil's when she joined us.

Other people were still passing along the path behind us, and

Hil said she might call it a night. I said I might stay, and she nodded and raised her arm in a Hil salute and said, 'Cheers then,' and strode away without looking back. After she had gone we sat down again. Michael folded his sweater and put it on the rock and patted it, and we sat next to each other while I told him how Hil had moved in with Stuart and me when I was five and stayed there until she bought the cottage around the corner, and how, later, when Stuart met his second wife, I had moved back in with Hil, and always seemed to return there. She was away most evenings anyway, I told him, at the Dump. Then I asked about his work and why he had chosen to be an anaesthetist and if he liked it, and after a moment he asked if I always talked this much and I said only when I was nervous and he said I didn't need to be, and then we sat for a long time in silence.

Bondi, which seems to me now unreal, like a smooth, sealed bubble on whose glistening surface everything is reflected back distorted. That was my life.

'Would you like to take a cushion?' said Anna, gesturing at the small pile in the corner of the room.

'Why?'

In answer, she walked across and picked up a smallish soft green pillow, then another in the same quiet tone of pink and held them both up by their corners.

'Which one?' she asked.

I shrugged and she said, 'Catch,' and threw me the pink one, which I grabbed and dropped, embarrassed, wishing already I had asked for green, which was less imbued with possible meaning. Anna crossed the room back to her chair, still carrying the green cushion, which she hugged up against her chest as she sat back cross-legged; arms, too, crossed in front of the pillow.

'What's it for?' I asked after a few seconds, leaning and picking mine up from the floor next to my seat.

'This,' she said, and hugged her pillow closer to her, as if it was something warm and precious. I knew what she was trying to do. I sat the cushion on my lap, and rested my folded hands on top of it.

Anna laughed. 'Try it,' she said. 'You might like it.'

'No thanks.'

'Why not?'

'Because it's silly.'

'Ah.' After a while she said, 'How's your week been, Jess?'

I told her it had been fine, not much happening, and then, because she just kept sitting there, head tilted very slightly to one side, I said that my father had rung last night and that we might be going bushwalking together one weekend after I got back.

'Where will you go?'

'I don't know. Maybe up around Newcastle where he lives. It might not happen.'

'Would you like to go bushwalking with your father?'

I shrugged. 'I don't know. I used to like it. We haven't been for a long time.'

Then I said that maybe I liked the idea more than the reality, and besides, what with Hil being up here so often, I probably had enough family to keep me going for now, more than enough, and then I stopped.

After a while I noticed I was stroking the pillow. Short, even strokes, as if it were a cat. I stopped and smoothed it, briefly, self-consciously, folded my hands again and kept talking. But before long I was stroking it again, the rough-textured cotton, the palm of my hand. I thought about stopping, and didn't. It was relaxing. I glanced up at Anna and she smiled.

'The pillow likes it,' I said by way of explanation. 'The

pillow finds it quite relaxing.'

'Lucky pillow,' said Anna.

'Yes.'

My father had crashed his car.

Some stupid bastard, he said, braking in front of him, except there was a cop driving past and the next thing he couldn't drive for six months.

It wasn't as if he was drunk either, he added. 'You know me, mate. Couple of glasses of red.'

And now Cassie wasn't speaking to him. There was a pause while I heard him uncork the bottle and pour himself another glass.

Eventually he asked how I was going, and I said fine.

'Really mate, how's it going? You back on your feet yet?'

I said it was going fine and I was doing a lot of walking, and I'd probably be ready to leave soon.

'Sorry mate,' he said, 'I've been a self-engrossed slob, Cassie's right, and I'm going to drive down this weekend and see you. It's bloody ridiculous, you're my child too, she'll just have to make the best of it. She can get her bloody mother down to help with the kids.' And then he remembered he didn't have a car, or a licence, and the conversation pretty much started again.

I didn't mind really. I didn't want anyone to visit. Not my father, not my husband. ('Poor bastard,' Steff muttered the second time I refused to take his call.) Some days not even Hil.

It was soothing though, listening to my father, familiar; his voice was pleasantly weighted, neither too light nor too heavy, and he required nothing of me. At school, my friends used to think it funny that he and Hil both called me mate, even when I was small.

But it was okay by me. I liked having a dad who would talk to me like a friend and tell me things that other dads didn't tell their daughters. Not that I think that any more; I'm just used to it. Part of me feels sorry for Cassie, even though she can barely bring herself to speak to me.

'She's just jealous, mate,' Stuart would say. 'Jealous of you, jealous of your mum.' As if it mattered.

I told him not to stress about the car, that I'd be out of there soon anyway, and that maybe we could grab a day, if we planned in advance, and go bushwalking, like old times. He said yes, he'd like that, in his normal voice, the one that he used to have, and I felt that he meant it, though I knew we wouldn't go.

'What do you do, Jess, when you want something?' asked Anna. 'Or when you don't. What do you do with wanting?'

'I don't know what you mean.'

'Just now, you said you wanted your aunt Hil not to visit as often. Is that right?'

'Well, sometimes I feel that, yes.'

'So what would you like her to do?'

'Well, I'd like her to do whatever she wants…be happy—' pause, 'and—'

'But what do you want, Jess?'

'You mean about her coming here?'

'Yes. What might you do about that?'

'Oh. Well, it's not just up to me—'

'Why not? Couldn't you tell her you don't want her to visit?'

'Oh, well, it's not that I don't want her to visit at all—'

'How often would you like her to visit?'

'Well she already visits less, after we spoke, after I talked to her.'

'So how often would you like her to come? What would be best for you?'

There was a longer pause.

'I'd like her not to come for a couple of weeks.'

'And do you think you could tell her that?'

'No.'

We sat down, facing each other, Anna and I, on cushions. 'What I would like you to do,' she said, 'is to put your hands against mine. Like this.'

We sat cross-legged, palms resting against each other. 'Now,' she said, 'I want you to push me away.'

I took my hands back. Put them in my lap.

'Come on Jess. Just give it a go.'

I put my palms to hers and my arms were full of black treacle. I pushed for a moment against her and the treacle seemed to run down into my shoulders, my ribs. I stopped.

'Try again,' she said.

I tried again but I didn't want to. I didn't want to push her away. I was shaking my head: I don't want to.

'Say the words, Jess. You are shaking your head. Say the words.'

No. I took back my hands and looked at her, not speaking.

'Okay. Let's try it another way. This time, I want you to pull me towards you. Like this.' And she grasped my fingers in hers and started to pull me. 'Come here,' she was saying, beseeching, a child. 'Come he-ere.' I snatched my hands away. 'Now you try,' said Anna.

I took a slow breath. My arms were crossed in front of me.

'See how you are hugging yourself,' she said, softly. 'You are protecting the heart.'

I nodded my head, slowly up and down, looking at her: I am protecting the heart.

After a minute I unwrapped my arms and held my hands again to hers. Our palms were warm against each other, a little moist. I looked at her because I couldn't find anywhere else to look. I tugged her towards me, once, with my hands, and stopped, still holding her fingers in mine. My arms were filled with syrup. I couldn't pull. I couldn't let her go. I could not speak. Please don't make me.

'Please,' I whispered.

It is quiet here in the space between thoughts. A jumbled clamorous quiet made of rustlings and clicks and the movement of air. In the silence my breath wells and wells and fills my hearing, the steady piston thump of my heart, so close to me, and beyond that other sensations that gradually differentiate into outlines of bird calls and cracking twigs and noises I cannot name. My mind looks for categories, a ceaseless scanning that separates wind and footfall and now cicadas, and keeps stretching further and further, seeking always the coding for threat: footsteps behind me, a rustling in the undergrowth. I must not die. I say it to myself over and over. I must not die.

Sometimes, when I know they will be out, I ring Sydney and listen to the answering machine. 'You have rung the house of Lily and Jess and Michael,' says my daughter's sweet clear voice. 'We're not home, but leave a message and we'll get back.'

My daughter, who is small and stern and about whom I will not think.

'Notice,' says Anna, 'how you touch your lips with your fingers. Notice how you soothe yourself.'

After a while I realise that I am whimpering. Small, curled sounds that are dislodged and shaken out of me with each step. At first I do not notice them, or name them anyway. At first it is just a feeling coiled in the back of my throat, not yet sound; another beat that falls in with the rhythm of my feet on the dirt road, softening and filling out my footsteps. For a moment when I hear the sound that I am making—when I realise that it is me making the sound—I stop. I tighten my throat and the sound stops. I wonder if anyone has heard. I walk more slowly. The crunch-shuffle of my boots on the road. The big empty air. And then I think, bugger it. And I soften my throat again, and pick up speed, and after a while it is back, a small animal following me, or leading.

It is odd at first, foolish. Babyish. But after a while I realise that it is a skill, an act of balance. The whimpering must neither be shouted over nor drawn in, contracted. In either case it loses its power to nourish, to alleviate. The whimpering must be left to its own devices, but held, my throat the cradle.

'I love,' says my husband suddenly, 'your large white breasts and your pale skin. I love all the things about you that you hate.'

At midday I stop for lunch. Hungry. I have been singing. Out here there is no audience, and if there is, they are welcome. I sing the

89

song I remember my mother singing with my father. A question and an answer.

'True love, true love, don't you lie to me. Tell me where did you sleep in the night?'

'In the pines, in the pines, where the sun never shines. And I shivered the whole night through.'

Most of the words I have forgotten, and I hum idly in between, improvising links and bridges, coming back over and over again to the same refrain. In the pines, in the pines, where the sun never shines. I am in the back of the car and my mother and father are in the front, singing together. I am sitting in the middle and from here I can see both of them, my mother on the left, the side of her face, her dark glasses, and my dad in the driving seat. He is sitting up straight, his big thin hands on the wheel, and his chin is tilted up, his wispy beard almost red in the last of the day's sunshine. He has a light tenor that brushes along beside my mother's deeper, stronger voice, and he looks so happy. I can see the happiness dancing around his skin.

I find a log in the shade, check it for ants and sit. I must be half way. At least half way. I still have two full bottles of water, and a half which I open now and swig, throat open. In my bag I have two muesli bars, a third of a bag of dried apricots, four tea-bags, one apple, two bananas, a block of chocolate, two packets of soup, bread, honey, marmalade and a vegemite sandwich. Not a lot, but enough. The sandwich, from the kitchen at the nursing home, is sweaty and limp now, the butter soaked into the bread. I hold it with both hands and eat slowly, the flavours and texture heightened by exertion. The bread, sourdough that Tina bought especially from the bakery, is chewy and yielding, the vegemite perfectly salty. I have a sudden powerful sense of wellbeing, the good fortune of my limbs and lungs which have brought me here, and through which blood and nutrients are coursing.

In the rec room, we bounced and shook. Maud, Elsie, Mary, Anna and I. Shaking and shuffling on the spot, laughing more easily now. 'Now yawn,' said Anna. 'Deeper. Deeper. That's right, right down to the diaphragm. Good, Jess. Now stretch. Remind the body we're still alive.'

'Tell that to my legs,' said Maud, glancing towards her stick, which she had left leaning against the wall. We were becoming familiar with each other, almost comfortable. Maud had been here for nearly a year, I now knew, since her second stroke, and although she was among the younger of the other residents she was wheezing slightly already. She had a soft broad back and plump shoulders, and wore floral print dresses without stockings. Sometimes she pulled her hem up and rubbed at her varicose veins.

'Four kids,' she announced, by way of explanation, 'and none of them gone off the rails, at least not yet,' as if this too were attributable to the dark knots behind her knees.

'It must have been very full-on,' said Anna, 'having so many children.' Sometimes she did this, I noticed, talked as if to a slightly younger audience she was trying to impress. Full-on. I wondered suddenly if she was doing it for my benefit. Maud looked for a moment as if she hadn't heard but then she nodded, with a slight smile, and said, 'That would be putting it mildly.'

Elsie—pale blue stretchy pant suit, hair to match—turned to Anna. 'Do you have children, dear?'

'Me,' said Anna, considering, 'no. No. Now today we're going to be monkeys.'

Anna stood at the front of the room and jutted her jaw out. She looked, it was true, like a monkey, the lower jaw pushed so far out that we could see her bottom teeth coming forward. She looked ridiculous. She retrieved her face for a moment and smiled. 'Easy,' she said, sticking her jaw out again. 'Now you try.' Her voice had a weird slightly stretched sound. I didn't like it. I slumped my shoulders. Anna ignored me.

One by one the others stuck out their bottom jaws, and eventually so did I.

'Right out,' said Anna.

Mary in her nylon shirt looked like a tiny lizard, all pink and purple frills. Maud looked like a grader. I started to laugh.

'You should look in the mirror,' she said.

'There are some things that are good to say with your jaw out like this,' continued Anna. 'This is what monkeys do when they are angry, this is what they do when they want to warn another monkey off, when they want to defend their territory and before they attack. That's why it feels so good to do.

'Go away!' she said suddenly. She looked like Popeye but her voice was gruff and for a moment she seemed almost frightening.

'Go away,' I said back to her, jaw jutting, surprising myself. 'Go away. Bugger off.'

It felt good. Silly, but good. 'Bugger off all of you,' I said now to everyone in the room. 'Leave me alone.'

'That's good,' said Anna and they all beamed back at me.

'Go to hell,' I said in my monkey voice. 'I'm really sick of this.'

'What are you sick of?' asked Anna, jaw still thrust out.

'I'm sick of doing this stupid exercise and I'm sick of people looking at me as though there's something wrong with me. So you can all get stuffed.'

This was a long speech, the longest I had made so far, and in the small silence that followed, I could feel a powerful surge of energy through my body, a rush of adrenaline, and in the background a tiny nub of concern. What was I saying? Who was I?

'Fantastic,' said Anna. 'You don't have to be here by the way. You're free to go.' She said it normally and quite cheerfully.

I stuck my jaw out again. 'But then I wouldn't get to play silly games like this and tell everyone to bugger off.'

'You might find that you can tell people to bugger off, even when you're not in here,' said Anna, matter-of-factly. They were all watching me now with interest.

Maud caught my eye and said, 'Yeah, you can tell me to bugger off any time you want. Won't make any difference, but feel free.'

Anna looked to Maud; 'Maud, put your jaw out again and tell us what you want us to do.'

Maud stuck her jaw out again, put her hands on her hips, and stood for a moment like king monkey on the top of a hill. She turned her head from side to side, and then said, 'You can all get fucked.'

I could feel the laughter racing through my body. Embarrassing, except that everyone else was laughing too. Elsie was cackling so much she had to grab at her crotch and then took herself off to the side of the room and a straight-backed chair. Even Maud had gone a surprised pink.

Gradually we all subsided. 'Let's lie down for the last few minutes,' said Anna, 'or sit.' She helped Maud lower herself to a chair, and then let Mary hold her arm as she sank to the ground, quiet now, not laughing.

Close your eyes, said Anna, and we lay there together in the room in the newly oriented silence, filled with breath and blood.

After a while Anna's voice said to come back now. Slowly we sat up. Mary saw me looking at her, and nodded her head. 'What about you dear?' she said. 'Do you have any children?'

For a moment there was silence. Then I said that yes, I had a daughter.

'Have you got a photo?' said Elsie, and I nodded and pulled my wallet from my back pocket and took out a photo of Lily at the beach last summer. She had an orange rubber ring around her middle and was smiling up at the camera all blonde and curls.

'Curls from her dad, colour from L'Oreal,' I said—a family joke—when they stopped oohing and aahing.

'When's she going to visit?' asked Elsie. 'When can we see her?' And again I paused. I could feel Anna watching me from across the room.

'You should bring her,' said Elsie at last. 'You should bring her here.' The other women agreed and when I glanced up at Anna she was looking at me, not nodding or smiling. Just looking, and I pulled myself up and said time to go. As I left the room she reached across and squeezed my shoulder softly.

At night I dreamed that I was swimming in the ocean with Anna. We were swimming to America and she was covered with a white greasy substance that was supposed to protect and keep her warm. I was freezing, though, I could feel my legs becoming weak and numb. Here, said Anna, just do this, and she whirled her arms and legs about like a dishwasher until the water around us was all warm and thick with grease and we floated along together like plankton.

This road is a corridor. Low scrubby eucalypts lean towards each other as if to create an arch. They are reaching for the sun, I know that, but I like the way they close above me. I like to feel that it is personal. There is a sandy bank running alongside the road. From it sprout low prickly shrubs, sharp grasses, small serrated banksias, blue-green saplings, dead broken sticks. In the middle of the roadway is a tiny lime green shoot, perhaps a centimetre high, a single stalk from which sprout upright pointed needles, like a Christmas tree. All along the stem, still caught between the branching leaves, is the sandy soil through which the seedling has pushed to get here. Sometimes I see the flash of small lizards in the undergrowth. Once, as I walk, I stop thinking. I stop making shapes, and for a long moment I feel air, trees, sunlight, birdcall and insects throb in unison around me, this great containing pulse. I do not feel alone. I feel free. Even when the moment has gone, I can still feel it in my belly and I think to myself: that was peace; I think that was peace. And then it fades.

One day Maud didn't turn up at Anna's class. 'Would you mind checking her room, Jess,' she asked. 'It's not like her not to be here.'

Upstairs, outside her door, thirty-six, I hesitated then knocked. I knocked again when she didn't answer. Probably on the loo. In the shower. On the phone. Dead. Say the word, then it won't happen.

Her blinds were still down and at first I couldn't make out anything except the shape of the bed to one side, and the large over-stuffed armchair she had brought from home. 'Maud?' She was probably still downstairs at breakfast. The room smelled of the lilac talcum powder she always used and the chemical underlay of medicines. She was not in her bed. She was on the floor. My foot connected quite solidly with some part of her and I staggered, regained my balance, and stood for a moment looking down at the shape that was Maud. I did not want to look at her face. The blanket was half off the bed, as if she had accidentally pulled it with her as she tried to crawl to the door. She must have been crawling. One leg was still bent up, one arm extended forward, like road kill. I didn't even check her breathing or her pulse. I dragged the blanket across to where she lay and pulled it up over her body, tucked it around her chin, felt her skin suddenly cold, stiff, her hair still soft, with the hairpin still tucking back some stray wisp.

For some reason I shut the door behind me, then ran down the corridor, silently down the stairs, past the room where Anna and the others must now have begun, towards Viv's office. My body not my own, an autonomous module that moved beside me, covering ground without pain or thought. It spoke to Viv for me, told

97

her what I had found. Confronted like this with the actuality of death, all of her resistance to it disappeared. She nodded once, as if to confirm what I had told her, rang the buzzer on her desk, spoke on the intercom to one of the nurses. 'Room thirty-six please. Straight away.' Took off her mauve-rimmed glasses and exchanged them for another pair. Shrugged off her cardigan, hung it on the arm of her chair and told me to lie down on her sofa until she got back. Her actions were smooth and efficient and strangely graceful. As if this was the moment, these were the moments, for which she had rehearsed all her life.

I did as she instructed and lay on the couch, staring through the window into the half-empty branches of the sickly elm and the silvery grey sky they held. It had rained a little overnight and the tops of the branches were stained in dark irregular blotches. I wondered if Maud had heard the sound of it falling, if she had taken comfort in that. I wondered what it was like for her now, all alone and cold.

Whenever anyone died, Viv would hold a little ceremony. Under the elm if it was not raining, otherwise in the rec room, where we gathered for Maud. Viv called it dying, and I liked her for this. Not 'passing away' or 'leaving us', or just 'passing', as Steff used to say. It always surprised me with Steff, this delicacy when it came to dying. Even her voice softened, or at least thinned out—'so and so passed last night'. Almost timid.

But Viv knew what to do. She was in her element. She honoured the dead with precision and the living with details, which is the most, I think, you can offer to either.

'Maud Kathleen Bernadette Flanagan died last night, in room

thirty-six, where she had stayed,' already the tense adjusted for Maud's new circumstances, 'for eleven months. She was seventy-three. Her birth certificate tells me she was born in Dublin. The doctor believes she died somewhere between three and five a.m., of a heart attack. Maud had already had two small strokes, as you may recall. She leaves behind her a daughter and three sons. Also grand-children, some of whom you will have met.

'Well then, thank-you for coming. There is a collection bowl on the table. Any donations will go towards flowers for her family. I'll advise you shortly when and where the funeral will be held.'

Afterwards a few of the others might get together in some-body's room with a bottle of sherry and share anecdotes or gossip. I don't know; I never went. But I always turned up for Viv's cere-monies, and I think she understood that I found them comforting. Sometimes she looked straight at me, not one of her usual skating glances. Sometimes she looked straight at me, and I at her, and I felt in this way that we were connected.

At the home I required of myself only one task each week. Every Wednesday now for more than a month, a letter has arrived from my daughter. She writes them on the weekend, at home with Michael, and on Monday, during a coffee break I suppose, Michael drops them at the post office in town. Normally she draws me a picture, which she folds over to make a card. Great reckless con-glomerates of colour, depicting I'm not sure what, driving the empty space from the page; inside, in her jaunty jostling script, she writes *Dear mummy*, embellished often with stars or hearts and sometimes fish, and then Michael takes over and variously transcribes: *I love you/ hope you are feeling better/ happy/ I am missing you/ I went to*

Carly/ Nathan/ Bim's house to play/ daddy bought me an ice-cream/ lolly/ I have built a castle in my room. I want to leave it up for you to see but daddy won't let me/ I am missing you/ missing you/ missing

It is a strategy of Michael's. Mean-hearted, I know, for me to see things this way, yet each week, I am certain, he has her decorate the envelope to be sure it will not end up in the drawer with the rest. And in each letter he inserts too a note from himself—determinedly chatty, giving details of callers (fewer) and outings (Manly with Hil) and general housekeeping (dripping tap on porch)—as if everything is all right, as if nothing has changed. Each lovingly adorned envelope a Trojan horse.

'It is true,' said Anna, 'that he is trying to keep you connected to your life with him and Lily.'

'But what can I do? He's using Lily to trap me.'

'Perhaps,' said Anna, 'you could use him to tell Lily a story.'

Each Wednesday at around four, ignoring the tightness in my chest, I made my way down to the front sitting room and settled myself in the blue armchair that looked out on to the side garden and, resting my paper on a book, I wrote my reply. I wrote her a story. I wrote about the little starfish whose mother had gone away on a journey.

In these stories, which evolved naturally, without thought, and which now number five, the mummy starfish must try to get back a black pearl that has been stolen from her by a frightening monster who lives in a giant clamshell on the bottom of the sea. The monster is called the Nuthing, and the mummy starfish is afraid of it. To get back her pearl she cannot walk straight up to the clamshell, or it will open up in a rush and the Nuthing will swallow her whole. Instead, the mummy starfish, whose name is Nancy, must work out sneaky ways to creep up on the monster and retrieve what is rightfully hers. Along the way Nancy starfish has adventures and meets various friendly and not so friendly creatures of the sea. Each week she asks the little starfish, whose name is Lily, to think of a spell or tricky scheme to help her open the clam and distract the monster while Nancy starfish gets the pearl. *Nancy should get a gun*, wrote my daughter, *and shoot the Nuthing/ She should use a bow and arrow/ She should leave a bowl of food to make the Nuthing come out of its shell*. So far though, while Nancy has found many useful things (a hamburger, a bent key, a large wooden nulla nulla with which to beat away her enemy), she has not been able to find what she has lost.

In the days after I sealed and posted my story I tried not to think about it again. I tried not to think about it again until Wednesday, when the mail arrived, and after I had read her letter (two, three times—I took it on my walk) I got a glass of water, went to the sitting room and settled myself in the blue chair. It was surprising how quickly the time passed. I never wanted to begin, but in the end, every time, it was a relief.

The first time I saw the man who would become my husband was through the glass door that led into the foyer at work. I was late, my tooth was aching and I was trying to open the door without putting down the box of books I was carrying. He was standing with his back to me, a slim figure looking at the magazines on the mantelpiece, and our eyes met briefly and precisely in the large mirror that hangs there, before he turned and walked across to open the door. I thanked him and said that Emma, who was now my boss, must have popped out for a minute.

'She's getting coffee,' he said. 'I'm early.'

He was still holding a book on childhood asthma, one we had published the previous year. He was dark—hair, eyes, suit—and quietly spoken. His movements were small and efficient (he closed the book quietly without glancing at it again and placed it on the low table). All this I noticed through the pain in my jaw as he carried the box of books into my room, where I had directed him. I couldn't stop looking at him. Later I realised that he rarely wore suits and must have been nervous, although it did not show. What I noticed was a sense of restraint that might or might not turn out to be shyness.

'Are you the one doing the anaesthesia book?' I asked.

'So it seems.' Oddly formal. 'I've got an outline here.'

'Good. I'll be editing it. We're always on the look-out for doctors who can write in English.'

He nodded.

'As opposed to Latin and jargon,' I explained, although he seemed not to get the joke, or not to find it funny.

He picked the asthma book up. 'Can I borrow?'

'Take it home and have a look. How's the writing going?'

'Good, I think, though it's hard to know how much to put in, how much information to give.'

'I told you, didn't I, that my husband was once awake during an operation?' said Em, who had just pushed open the door, balancing three coffees and a couple of muffins. 'He couldn't move or feel anything, but he heard everything. It was like he was stuck.'

Michael held the door for her and took a cup, which he handed to me.

'No thanks, I've got a toothache.'

'He could hear the surgeon,' said Em, 'or whoever it was, talking about the cricket score. Andrew was really annoyed. He's a Pom and Australia was winning.'

'Yes, that happens sometimes,' said Michael. 'Hearing's the last sense to go.' He turned to me. 'Have you got a good dentist?'

I said I had an appointment for that afternoon, and he nodded and moved to follow Em into her office. Just as he entered he turned back to me. 'Here,' he said, and fumbled with his black leather satchel before passing me a sleeve of white tablets, 'take two of these.'

After he went, I looked up the *Oxford English Dictionary*. *Anaesthetise*, it said, *render insensible*.

Among the books on the shelf above my desk at work were the Macquarie Dictionary (of Australian English), the Oxford English, *Roget's Thesaurus of Synonyms and Antonyms*, Strunk and White, and Fowler's *Modern English Usage*. Just looking at their solid spines above me made me feel calm. 'If the answer's not there,' I used to tell writers, gesturing at the bookshelf, 'I give up or make it up.' But they always were there. They always are. Mixed metaphors, split infinitives. Dangling participles (Fowler prefers to call them unattached), in which the two parts of the sentence don't match. 'Surprised and pleased, her tooth seemed to ache less immediately.' The surprised tooth. Confusion about the subject.

A week later he walked past me as I was waiting for my bus. He was on the way to his car. It was a casual exchange of pleasantries that created its own force field, neither of us implicated by more than circumstance, and kept us talking there, first standing, then leaning together against the bus shelter, for the ten minutes it took for the bus to come. He asked me about my work, not out of politeness, it seemed, but interest—not in the material published, but in the process of editing.

'How do you decide what to take out and what to leave in?'

'Well—' slow at first, trying to gauge his level of interest, how much he really wanted to know. 'You take out anything that is not necessary.' I paused, and glanced at him quickly, aware that I had put more thought than must seem necessary into a statement so obvious. I waited for him to laugh or turn away. But he asked again, focused, insistent, 'But how do you know what is necessary? How do you make that decision? How do you decide what it is that matters?'

'It matters if it is interesting,' I said at last. 'That is the first thing. It matters that the information is of value.'

I stopped again, wondering when he would be sick of this, but he was nodding his head, small precise punctuations.

'It matters that it is clear, that it is intelligible. It matters that it is to the point.' I paused. 'Though that can be open to negotiation. Sometimes something may not seem immediately relevant, but you feel that it's important, so you try to work out where it fits and why.'

And now he smiled just slightly. 'So there is some room for negotiation?' And I smiled slightly back, and said, 'A little. Not too much.' From the corner of my eye I could see my bus further down the street and I knew that this was the natural place to end the conversation, the hint of gentle sparring, a small realignment, but I said quickly, because it was what had occurred to me and because the information seemed to me interesting, of value, 'What is harder than knowing what to take out, is knowing what is missing. That is the hardest part.'

The bus was nearly here, he had heard it too, and we straightened together. I pulled my bag higher on my shoulder, the slight awkwardness of finishing. 'I'd like to talk more about this,' he said. I nodded vigorously, too vigorously probably, I thought later, but he did not seem uncomfortable, at least no more so than I, and he waited while the bus door shut and I found a seat—at least he was still there when I turned to look through the window—and raised his arm briefly before turning and walking off.

The next day at work I asked Em about his manuscript, casually, and when it might be ready for me to look at.

'You can have a look at a draft now if you like,' she said, passing it over. 'He says he'll get the final version to me in a fortnight or so—we've got another meeting—and after that he's all yours.'

I wonder now how Emma is managing, if she has someone doing my job. She came to see me at the nursing home once after I woke up. She wore her red lipstick and her shiny black boots with zips up the sides. She brought magazines. *Vogue, Newsweek, Vanity Fair, Who.* We were downstairs in the sitting room and her voice was too loud. Old people, even deaf people, turned to look at her. I could not hold a thought. I could not follow the trail of her thoughts. They flapped around like streamers, red and yellow and blue, and became tangled, until I stopped listening.

'Look,' I said, and I pointed out the window. 'There are my birds.' It was the first time I had seen them from any window but mine, and I thought how much I appreciated their greyness, grey shapes in a white sky, and how, up close, there would be mauve and soft brown and sedate creamy tips on some of the feathers. This is why I am here, I thought. I felt a wave of such tiredness that after another minute I excused myself. I did not ask her up to my room, and though we hugged at the door I knew that I had not given her what she wanted. Nor she me. I left the magazines downstairs on the table and did not look at them again. After that I told Viv I did not want visitors, except Hil. Emma rang a couple of times (I found the messages on my bed) but she did not try to visit, and I knew that she had got the message and that she would get on, for now, without me.

I took his manuscript home and read it in the bath, careful not to splash stray drops of water that might mark the paper or cause the print to run. 'One hundred and fifty-four years after a Boston dentist called Thomas Morton gave the first successful public demonstration of what is now known as surgical anaesthesia,' he wrote, 'we still don't know exactly how anaesthetics work. We know that a general anaesthetic acts on the central nervous system—reacting with the membranes of the nerve cells in the brain to shut down responses such as sight, touch and awareness—but the precise mechanisms and effects remain uncertain.'

Dr Michael Small, whose sentences had a steady forward momentum, and whose participles did not dangle.

It was two weeks or more before I saw him again—he was walking into Emma's office as I was walking out of mine—by which time I was sick of thinking about him. In the days after the bus stop talk, I had run the conversation in a loop through my head. Replayed over and again the feeling of his earnest engagement; the smile when he had said, 'So there is some room for negotiation?'; the image of him standing at the bus stop, hand raised in farewell. I knew it was not wise, I knew it was bad luck, but I'd allowed myself even to imagine, just briefly, what it would be like to kiss him, the soft pads of our lips, the subtle, moist negotiations. I'd replayed the images and imaginings until I had sapped the juice from them, until they were husks, and the thought of them produced only dissatisfaction, a slight nausea. So the first feeling I had, alongside the thud of excitement at finding myself standing in front of him in the office, was irritation, a sense that he had somehow let me down. And it was this feeling, or the fear that he would recognise this feeling, that kept me walking past him, barely pausing to snap him a sharp quick smile, eyebrows raised, before heading for the kitchen, where I closed my eyes and leaned my face against the side of the fridge in disgust.

I waited for a few minutes, dawdling over the tea, hoping that he might on a sudden impulse come in and find me there. But he didn't and I spent the next hour at my desk fighting off sad, heavy feelings and toying distractedly with a manuscript that had arrived that day about Aboriginal health, or the lack of it.

Normally I wouldn't have bothered. It was not a book we would ever publish. There was a story at the start about a woman returning to the top-end community she had been taken from when she was nine. I read it more through inertia than anything else. It was a familiar enough tale: the government people arriving, the kids being rounded up and put on the truck, everybody crying. Em had left her door a little open and now and then I could catch a voice (his) or laughter (hers) from inside her office. One young mother had tried to make a bolt for it, but on being cornered had run back to the truck and thrust her baby into the arms of the nine-year-old, made her promise to look after it. No surprise to read that soon after they got to the children's home near Darwin, a white couple came and took the baby away. Eventually I let myself realise that I was hungry and that the reason I was not eating was that I didn't want to miss him leaving. And after that it was not so difficult to rise, take my jacket from the back of my door and head out of the office without lingering. As I paused at the bottom of the wooden steps to check in my bag for my wallet, Michael opened the door behind me and came down the steps.

'Hello. Are you having lunch? Do you want to get something to eat?'

I said sure, which seemed easy, and we walked in a serviceable silence together down the street.

The cafe did not feel so easy. He had clearly defined, cherubic lips, and I could not remember where on a face to look to be natural. We sat at the only free table, too close to the door, so that people passing in and out brushed past us with their jackets and bags and a couple of times we both reached protectively for the bottle of water. The second time, Michael picked it up and moved it to the other side of the table and I thought, that is what I should have done. Now he will think I lack initiative.

A woman entered, dragging a small blond boy by the wrist. She leaned over the counter next to us and shouted queries at the man who was frothing milk for coffees in a jug.

'I need a table for four. When will there be a table?' The coffee man kept frothing the milk but pulled an enquiring look over the jug.

'Hang on,' he mouthed. The woman kept shouting.

'How long will we have to wait for a table? When will it be quieter in here?'

I winced, slightly, comically, in her direction, but Michael, next to her, seemed not to notice.

He had soft, dark curls and deep set eyes which darted quickly around the room before stopping very still. I had the sense that he was waiting for something. I wondered if he was going to ask me about my work; if he had thought about me since the bus stop talk.

We looked at the menu and made small talk while we waited to order. I said the toasted sandwiches were good. Michael said he knew, he had come here once with Emma, though not at lunchtime and now he knew why. I asked if he lived around there, and he said no, he lived in Bondi. 'Me too,' I said. Trying not to sound too pleased. Instead I started to tell him about the kitchen at Hil's house; the bird table I had helped her build outside the window, and the rosellas that were now tame enough to eat from your hand. Some days, I said, I came home and the garden was full of kids and birds. I added that it was a small garden, mostly taken up by a fig tree, and that it only took a few kids to fill it. But that these kids had never known much tenderness, yet they sat so still there with Hil, husky voices lowered, arms outstretched, waiting.

I spoke without looking at him, and although everything I said was true I was aware that I was telling the story for my own purposes and that those purposes were obscure even to me. I spoke partly, I knew, in order not to look at him. In order not to have to keep wondering if I mattered to him. I told him a story about myself in order to hide from his scrutiny. But I chose to use that word tenderness—and the image of the waiting children. Then I stopped and there was nothing more to say and still I could not look at him, so I ran my gaze around the cafe's blue and white interior and saw that the woman with the blond child had found a table and was sitting there with a blond man and the child and another, older, child, a girl.

I wondered if they were a family.

'What do you do Jess,' says Anna, 'when you want something?'

*

After a while he asked how long I had been a copy editor. I said three or four years I supposed; it had sort of crept up on me. 'It suits you,' he said. 'You look like a copy editor.'

I said it must be the glasses, which were round and dark. He said, yes, and the hair—which back then was short and white.

'You look like a doctor,' I said, 'but I won't hold it against you.'

I told him then about the manuscript I had been reading, and about how thirty years later she had gone back, the nine-year-old who had been taken away, to try and find her family. How she had arrived in the middle of the day and walked along the dirt road towards a group of Aboriginal people sitting in the shade of a tin-roofed shed; how suddenly a figure had detached itself from the group and started running towards her. It was an old woman and her arms were stretched out in front of her and when she reached the woman who had returned, she said, 'You got my baby? Where my baby?'

As I talked, Michael watched me with his dark eyes and nodded slowly.

I asked him then if anaesthetics could be dangerous, and he gestured towards the knife with which I was buttering my roll, and said anything could be dangerous if it wasn't used properly; they were powerful drugs. There was a bit of an art, he added, to knowing just how much of the drug to give. That was what made a good anaesthetist. There were guidelines of course, but every patient was different. Also, it depended how deep you wanted them to go. Sometimes, he said, if someone was terribly wounded, he might put them in a coma, an anaesthetic coma, to give the body a chance to heal. Sometimes the only way to save someone from death was to take them part of the way there.

Up here, the trees rise from a bed of rock, moulded basalt that follows the earth's contours, creating lips and ledges where the soil has washed away beneath it. Even in the charred rock there is nourishment; lichens in pale greens and deep rust reds colonise the surface and in every gap and hollow, earth has formed from which grasses and other small plants reach out. Sometimes I come across small groups of trees or shrubs where there seems to be no life. But even here if I look close I find tiny green shoots, right at the base, beginning to push through.

I was fascinated by his hands, the long square-tipped fingers, which he moved as he talked, and the smooth splayed nails. Mine, which I bit, I kept folded beneath my palms on the table, two vague fists. I wondered if he kept his like this for his patients. It seemed oddly flawed, I said at last, to need that amount of guesswork. Not like science. Not like grammar. More like sleep, I thought, which might come or might not. 'Sometimes,' I said, 'I fantasise about snakes and squirrels and other animals that hibernate. I sometimes wish I could do that.' And then I felt foolish because he did not answer and kept staring beyond me, as if I had not spoken.

Sometimes it seemed to me that the times I felt the most myself were at work, when I was editing: the fluid, formal arrangements of commas, full stops and semicolons, the precise unarguable shifts in meaning; sentences and paragraphs rearranged, ideas corralled, collated; excised.

'That's how I felt when I split up from my wife,' he said

suddenly. 'I stopped sleeping. I'd sleep maybe two or three hours a night. It was weird. I wasn't tired. In the morning I'd get up and go to work, and I was fine. I seemed fine. And as soon as I got home I'd just go to bed. I'd lie there for hours and hours and hours. I'd get tranquilisers from work, but I couldn't sleep. I would have given anything to sleep.'

The subtle, unarguable adjustment of rhythm and flow.

At the end of the meal we ordered takeaway coffees and then walked back to the office where, instead of parting, we sat, as if it were already habit, on the concrete steps. I wanted to ask about his wife, and when she had left. 'Do you think people can know anything,' I asked, 'when they're unconscious? Emma's mum, when Em was doing exams, she used to sit by her bed until she'd gone to sleep and then she'd read to her from her swot notes. Em's convinced it was what got her through.'

'No,' he said, shrugging. 'I don't think so. Anaesthesia's not sleep. People sometimes say they heard stuff, but mostly it's dreams.' Occasionally, though, he said, someone would start to wake before you wanted them to. The other day, he said, a bloke had tried to sit up while they were still stitching him and they'd had to give him more propofol to settle him down. 'Although we might not mention that in the book,' he said. And we both smiled.

What about the man, though, I asked: would he remember?

Michael said no; the drugs made you forget.

The backpack is pressing into my shoulders, sending lines of sensation up both sides of my neck each time I step. It is heavy, heavier than I had imagined at the shop. It takes more energy than I had expected just to walk. I stop and adjust the hip strap, tightening it properly so that it rests now on my hip bones, which I can feel taking the weight, releasing the pressure on my back. I think of the brown leather satchel Hil bought me as a present when I started school. The silver buckles that she adjusted over my chest. My pencil case, my drink bottle, my lunch in a paper bag, sandwiches wrapped in greaseproof paper. How I would wait out the front after school for her to come and get me, and how each day I would imagine that instead of Hil standing by the gate, it would be my mother waiting there in the old Holden. I tried not to think it, but I always did. And each time I thought it, I felt guilty.

'But the body,' I want to say to Michael. 'What about the body? Does the body remember?'

'For an editor,' said Michael, 'you have terrible handwriting.'

It is true. Everything in my writing is designed to conceal, to make sure that the person next to me cannot see into my mind. I write so fast I miss some letters and distort others so completely that reading it back five or ten minutes later whole words are unrecognisable, even to me.

'I think I might have to get you a proper pen,' said Michael the first time we worked together in my office, looking over the notes for his book. And he did: a long silver one on a velvet bed. He brought it to our next meeting. I was not sure what to make of it, of the fact of him giving it to me. I was not sure whether to take it as a gift, signifying something, or just as the sort of thing he did, the sort of thing he would do for his friends, a wholesome, practical thing. But was I a friend?

Sometimes when I write I feel that I am skating, that the pen is skating across the page and that I am on thin ice. And then I pull myself up, slow down, start again. It is safer to work with other people's words, to order and reveal the thoughts of others.

'If you put this bit up here,' I said to Michael, 'then you don't need that sentence in between. You don't need to tell us those two thoughts are connected, because you've already connected them. Do you see?'

As I am walking I pick up a small yellow stone and put it in my mouth. I do not intend to. It is a soft pinky yellow, quartz-like and smooth, a pebble really, with rounded edges. Everything is so clean up here. I put it to the tip of my tongue and lick, and then, because there is no one here and because it is cool and somehow pleasing, I put it in my mouth. It feels odd on my tongue, surprising at first and colder than me, tasting slightly of dust, though it soon becomes warm and I find that I can tuck it to the side of my mouth, alongside the jaw, and that the soft clack clack against my teeth is companionable. After a while I see another pebble and another, and soon I am walking along with a mouth full of stones, five or six tucked behind my teeth or beneath my tongue. I can move them around together or separately, creating small migratory groupings and helping my body to produce saliva. It feels as if my back teeth have fallen out and are rolling around inside my head.

The first time we went out together, we passed an accident as we came out of Bondi. There was a car on its roof. Michael drove past and then slowed. He said, 'Shit; there's no ambulance.' He pulled over and told me to wait in the car. After he left I turned on the radio. When he came back about twenty minutes later he had blood on his hands and his face and shirt. He asked if I would mind driving us to his flat, and I saw that his hands were shaking.

'That,' he said in tight voice, 'is what I hate most about being a doctor. That is why I chose to be an anaesthetist.'

I drove him home, uncertain what to say or how to comfort, and after he had showered and changed we ended up walking up the street and getting pizza. I asked if he had always wanted to be a doctor. He said he didn't know, he supposed so, his father had been, but he had died quite young.

Later, over margherita and red wine, he told me that the man in the car had died while they were waiting for the ambulance. I didn't know what to say. Eventually I said, 'At least you were there with him.' Michael shrugged and started to say something then stopped. After a while he said he still remembered the first time he had put someone to sleep, a middle-aged woman having a lump removed from her breast. She was wheeled in awake. He had not met her before, he was only a trainee, under supervision. But he was the one who anaesthetised her. He attached the monitors to measure blood pressure, pulse, the amount of oxygen in the blood, and found that it was easy to chat to her lightly, soothingly. She was nervous of course, pale and awkward, lying on her back in the ugly hospital gown, trying to smile when she was spoken to, nodding at his questions. She had put on lipstick. He felt sorry for her, and suddenly, to his surprise, terribly protective. He asked about her children. Her son was eighteen and thinking about doing medicine. He kept talking while he took her right arm, rubbed a numbing agent in the soft crook, then the local anaesthetic. 'Just a small prick coming up, that's it, perfect. It's a bit of an odd feeling isn't it?' and then connecting her to the drip. 'And what about your daughter?'

She started to answer, got out maybe half a dozen words, and then smiled and breathed in as if she had just remembered something, and that was all. He looked down at her and thought, 'I did that', and tucked her arm up against her body where it would stay warm.

'It's kind of silly really,' he told me, shrugging. 'It's not as if she'd be feeling the cold.'

And then he added: 'I was talking to a forensic pathologist once. He was doing some work at the hospital. Funny guy. Really funny guy. He told me you can always tell if it's a domestic, you know, if it was someone who loved them. They put a blanket over the body or a pillow under their head.'

And then he said, 'I like you. I like you a lot.'

It was a few weeks after that that I paid my visit to the psychiatrist in Potts Point. I didn't tell Michael I had gone. I had not yet moved into his tiny flat, and besides, there was not much to tell, although afterwards I tried to write about it. 'On my fifth birthday we went on a picnic in teh mountains,' I typed on my laptop on the back steps at Hil's. I stopped, pulled myself up, took myself back, changed 'teh' to 'the'. Reread: 'On my fifth birthday we went on a picnic in the mountains.' On my fifth birthday we went on a picnic. I went blank. I wondered if he would love me. 'Do your first draft in a rush,' I had told him that first time we sat down together to work. 'Don't worry too much about spelling, punctuation, just get down the shape that's in your mind. You can fill in the gaps later.' But what, I thought, if you wrote so fast your fingers got ahead of your mind, what if you didn't know what was coming?

It was wrong, I knew, to think this way. I didn't even tell Emma. (What if something took you unawares?) On my fifth birthday we went on a picnic in the mountains. Full stop. And now what? Always the urge to go back, to adjust, to alter. To change teh to the. To interrogate. It didn't matter, I told myself, it didn't matter; just write. But it did matter. It was a blemish. And always this sense that if I didn't get it right now, if I didn't make amends straight away, that somehow I would never be able to undo it; that some pathway would have been created that I would be unable to change, to which I would return time and again, reinforcing and deepening it. That I would be trapped forever in my own error. Teh. Something misplaced.

Dear mummy, writes Lily, *Nancy starfish should feed the Nuthing a poison fish.*

The first time I saw Michael naked I thought of potters' clay, fine-grained and whitish, and I had the sense that if I were to press my thumb against his flesh he might not rise back, but might stay like that always, moulded. It was an impression only, fleeting, at odds with the taut, tanned arms and runner's legs, but when I think of him it is what I see. It is there too around the corners of his mouth and eyes, where the expression seems always to hover just beyond his features, felt rather than seen. As if someone forgot to apply the final layer and now he is vulnerable to the elements, to leaching and evaporation. So that when he looks at you, when he looked at me, the exchange was glancing, momentary, and the contact seemed to take place in the space between us, neither forming nor dissipating. So that even now, even when he is not here, he seems to fill the air with his unspoken, inexact requirements. And I am never free of him.

There is a blister on the sole of my left foot, a pinkish bubble far beneath the surface. I noticed it this morning when I put on my boots, and now it provides a steady bass beat as I walk. In my first aid kit I have Panadol, antiseptic cream, band-aids, a sealed wound dressing, two plastic syringes of distilled water and two bandages which you could use to stem the flow of blood, or if you were bitten by a snake. These days they tell you not to use tourniquets. If you are bitten you wrap the bandage with a firm, even pressure along the wounded limb (bad luck if it's your neck, I think), not too tight or you cut off the blood supply. If the blood cannot get to the tissue, the tissue starts to die. People have lost limbs. You use a firm, even pressure to slow the movement of the toxins through your body. You keep the limb as still as possible and get to a hospital. If you can, you give the doctors a clear description of the snake, its shape and size and colouring, so that they can find the antidote.

Venom. Antivenene. From Latin *venenum* poison, love potion, related to *venus* sexual love.

Anna nodded almost gravely as I came in, then smiled. 'Sit down,' she said. Her voice seemed increasingly deep, melodious. I glanced at her quickly. Her hair was short, wavy. Tousled. Sweet smelling. 'How are you Jess?' A slight upwards inflection.

I was not sure how I was. First I said, 'Fine, I'm fine,' and found myself gazing over her head and to the right to the books on the shelves. Then, still not looking at her, I said quickly, 'Actually, I'm not exactly fine. I feel a bit, I don't know, agitated. I'd been feeling quite calm, quite good. And now I don't. I keep having dreams. And thoughts. My brain won't stop.'

I glanced at her. 'Last time after I saw you, I got quite teary. And exhausted. I was meant to see my aunt Hil the next day, and I couldn't. I was too tired. I had to cancel, and I spent the day in bed. So, I'm okay now though.' I trailed off, brought my eyes back to her, then away. 'Though I've got a bit of a headache.'

'Where does your head hurt?'

'Oh, just at the back, a bit, it's fine. I'll take a Panadol.'

'Your neck?'

'Yes, in the back of my neck.'

'Why don't we do some work on the back of your neck then?'

Leaning against the far wall was a small foam mattress. Anna picked it up and carried it to the centre of the room. I should help her, I thought, but I felt clumsy, ineffectual. And nervous. What did she want?

'Lie,' she said, 'on your back.' She knelt at my head. The room looked different from this angle, the creamy paint unembellished, unwelcoming. I was aware of her sitting behind me. If I tilted my head a little I would be looking at her. I closed my eyes and she put her hands to my shoulders, working the muscles with her fingers, moving towards the base of my skull.

'Oof. No wonder you have a headache.' We laughed, and I relaxed a little. In my mind's eye I saw her thumbs pushing into my flesh, releasing colours. Lines of brilliant red and green.

'Jess?' She was asking me something.

'Mm?'

She wanted to know if I was comfortable. I opened my eyes

for a moment and saw her leaning above me, upside down. She was enormous. Her hair had fallen forwards. She eclipsed the ceiling. I closed my eyes, dropped down and down into my body, plumb lines from her fingers. After a while I realised that my legs were hot and heavy, a strange burning sensation. Anna spoke again. She said, 'Jess, how are you going?'

I was trying to answer her. I was trying to tell her it didn't feel quite right. Something was not quite right. I was trying to tell her that my legs felt strange and lost and empty. I remembered instead a trip to the doctor's with Stuart. I am sitting on the raised bed with my legs outstretched. The doctor has grey hair and a suit that smells of cigarettes. 'There is no reason why she shouldn't be walking,' he tells Stuart. His voice is quite kind. 'There is nothing wrong with her that we can see.'

'Jess?'

I opened my eyes. I looked at the ceiling. 'How are you going there, sweetheart?' Anna.

'Okay. My legs feel funny.'

I didn't mind that she called me sweetheart. Her voice was broad and soft and reassuring.

'Do you want to get up?'

'No. Yes. No.'

'Which one?' She laughed.

'I think I need to stand. My legs feel sort of buzzy. Tickly.'

I wanted suddenly to stamp my feet. I wanted to stamp them hard on the floor. I wanted to say, 'Anna, I think I need to stamp. Can I stamp?' But I didn't know how to ask. I said, 'My feet feel tickly, as if I need to stamp them.'

'Good,' said Anna. 'Then stamp.'

At first I felt foolish. I felt like an actor. I felt that I was wearing galoshes. I was not so much stamping as clumping my way around the room. Boomp boomp boomp as my feet hit the floor. But my feet liked it. With each step the tingling feeling came rushing back up my legs. It made me want to laugh. And suddenly, just like that, I was stamping my right foot, really hard, bang bang bang, into the floor, like a buck rabbit. I stopped at three because I knew I still could. And because I wanted to shout; my mouth wanted to shout, and I didn't want it to. I was scared of what would come out.

'Keep going,' said Anna, calmly, encouragingly. 'You're doing really well.'

I wanted to help her. I wanted to do as she had asked. But my throat closed over. All the energy seemed to drain back down into the floor. I shut my eyes and shook my head. 'I'm sorry.'

'There's nothing to be sorry about, Jess. That's good work. Would you like to lie down again?'

On the mattress, I lay on my side and she sat behind me. She put one cool hand to my forehead. 'Is it all right if I stroke your head?' I nodded, yes, and she stroked my hair back from my fore-head. 'You did really well, sweetheart.' Still stroking.

Later, alone in my room, I put my hand to my forehead, felt the coolness of my fingers, how my face rested into them, nudged gently as I stroked the hair back from my forehead. Sweetheart.

I woke while it was dark, a breeze flapping the blind against the open window, and thought again about the grey-haired doctor talking to Stuart.

'There's a—' he pauses, '—doctor you could see in the city who's good with this sort of thing. Otherwise—I'd give it time. She's had a shock. Time is a surprisingly good healer.' Stuart carries me out. As we leave, the doctor hands me a barley sugar wrapped in coloured cellophane. 'You be a good girl,' he tells me, 'and get better for your daddy.'

All the next day and the days after that, I thought about Anna. I wanted to touch her.

It was a month or so before I saw where Michael worked. When he was not teaching, he spent half his time on the third floor of the hospital.

'Come on up,' his voice said the first time I visited, when the receptionist buzzed him from the shiny new lobby, 'I'll be through in a few minutes.'

Away from the lobby the building stretched in all directions in endless, fluorescent corridors with green linoleum and round institutional clocks. From the lift, I followed the signs to obstetrics and spoke through a sliding glass window to a woman I took to be a nurse, who then opened the door marked staff only and let me in.

'Michael will be right out,' she said in a friendly voice, and asked me to take a seat on one of the orange benches. I didn't recognise him when he came. He was dressed from head to toe in green, his hair beneath a cap, face hidden by a mask. Even his shoes were covered with soft fabric slippers. When the door beside me opened all I noticed, with an obscure shock of recognition, was the brief wedge of lights and stainless steel beyond, and a momentary impression of a trolley and green-clad human forms moving around it; a cheerfully raised female voice. Then the door closed again, and the man standing next to me pulled down his face mask, and even then it took a moment—the hair still covered—to realise it was Michael. He smiled distractedly and ruffled the back of my hair.

'I'll just be a few more minutes. It's taking a bit longer than we expected. You okay here for ten minutes?' I nodded yes and smiled back. He turned and the door opened again briefly on to the operating theatre, which was familiar, I realised now, only from the television. Then he was gone. We hadn't kissed, and while this seemed apt, it added to my sense of disjunction. I wondered why it was taking longer than expected in there, whether there had been some medical emergency. I wondered if the brown mark on the front of his gown was blood. It occurred to me that although he had told me he was an anaesthetist and worked three days of every week in surgery, I had come here expecting to find him in an office, behind a computer. And that in his green garb, appearing from that brightly lit room beyond the metal door, he seemed to me irretrievably foreign.

Up ahead the road doubles back on itself in a long sharp hairpin bend. To my left is a shortcut, a steep rocky section of track, dirt and stone winding up between outcrops towards a stand of trees and the road high above. It could save me a kilometre, perhaps more. The cloud has cleared and although it is probably not all that hot, twenty-seven, perhaps twenty-eight degrees, the sun has a sharp edge. I pause at the bottom for a moment, thirsty, looking up. Then I start climbing without stopping for a drink or thought. I can feel the strain almost immediately in my legs, the backs of my calves, my buttocks. My feet are either angled sharply upwards or I am taking giant steps, pulling myself, my weight and the pack's, up between chunks of rock.

It is harder than it looks, each step requiring concentration, attention, the clenching of muscle, my forward momentum offset by the weight of the pack. My hands scrabble for holds. I can feel new sweat prickling on to my back, trapped by the pack, senseless wasted moisture. No chance of evaporation in there, just a dull build-up of heat. Cheap pack. Almost immediately, it seems, my breathing is ragged, mouth dry, blood thumping in my ears. Keep looking down. Watch my feet. My breath tastes like dry grey dust. Great gobs of it tearing into my lungs, the breathing and the earth the same now, unbearable. When I look up along the jagged line of the incline, it looks like a cliff face. Impossible.

I raise a hand to wipe my face and instead scrape my arm against a pointed outcrop, prickles of pain in a line from my elbow towards my wrist. Flash of hot feeling, anger, a sharp spike, and I take the next step too fast, wilfully careless, feel my foot wedge between rocks, my body swivel (see, you are about to be hurt), the pack catch against something—vegetable, mineral. An acid rush of adrenaline, a pain in my ankle as I teeter for a moment before grabbing on to a small spiky bush—which holds.

My body-mind stills instantly, ceasing to struggle, letting it all settle before assessing the damage.

Consequences: this is a consequence of that—of the moment when my anger twisted back on itself. I am lucky; the pain is not bad. My foot is still wedged, and I move carefully, kneeling on the other leg, using both hands to help raise my calf, ease the shoe from where it is stuck between rocks. I am calmer now, my body slow in the aftermath of the fright, respectful again. I sit, the straps of the backpack still on my shoulders, the weight resting on a ledge.

Now that it is over and I am safe, all I can feel around me is emptiness. I am in a vacant hollow of day. Unhurt, but despite myself. The sun beats and flares with my slowing pulse but I feel it darkly, cold now against my skin. My legs feel distant and unreal. I pull my drink bottle out, swallow without thirst or taste—the body's needs not yet reasserted—placating some grim watcher. See, I am drinking water. I am taking care.

It is only as I start to move that I feel the heat come back, the buzzing in my thighs. It is shock, I think; I must have had a bit of a shock; the coldness. I say it to myself again as I begin, carefully, evenly, to climb. Just a bit of a shock.

I reach the top quite quickly after that and sit, legs dangling against the warm rocks, the mind's clatter quieter for now. In the settling ripples of my near-accident my husband floats back into view, some distance off, in his running shorts.

Every day at the same time Michael runs, the same run every time, around the ocean path to Bronte and back—with a monitor strapped to his chest measuring distance, pulse rate, spent kilojoules. Before we had Lily, I used to sit and watch him from my table at the cafe as he finished. Checking his time, stretching his slender, finely muscled legs, and then leaping from the boardwalk to the beach, running into the ocean, fifty metres in, fifty metres out, shaking his head, water flying from his dark curls.

'Have you always been this obsessive?' I asked one day, early on, when he arrived back. He bent forward as if for a kiss, then rubbed his morning stubble across my chin instead.

'Oh piss off,' I said, pushing him away.

'But I love you.' He puckered his lips and leaned towards me, crossing his eyes.

'Yuk. Michael. Go away.'

He stopped and sat down next to me. Looked at me intently. 'Really?'

'Really? No.'

'I will. If that's what you want.'

'It's not.' I wrinkled my nose and looked down at the menu. 'Have the pikelets. The pikelets are good.'

'But maybe it is,' he said.

I looked up again. 'It's not.' I reached my hand out to touch his cheek, but he jerked his head back, staring at me.

'Michael?'

'Maybe it is, and that's why you said it.'

'Maybe I was joking, Michael.'

'Maybe this is all getting a bit much,' he said, half rising, 'all going a bit fast.'

He knocked the table with his knee, spilling hot coffee over my leg. 'Sorry, sorry,' he grabbed at a pile of serviettes and thrust them towards me, swiping at the stain. Then he sat back suddenly in his seat, dropped his head into his hands. After a few moments I reached out and tentatively touched the dark wavy hair. Without looking up he grabbed one of my fingers and held it tightly against his skull.

'Michael,' I whispered. He looked up. His eyes were wet. 'Michael, what's wrong?' I said. 'What's the matter?' He pulled me towards him then. His lips were cool and salty. I could feel his heart in his chest. The waiter had to rap on the table with his knuckles: 'Scuse me folks, this is a family restaurant.'

Michael pulled back. 'Sorry,' he said, looking at me. 'Sorry, I'm sorry, I'm sorry.'

'It's all right,' I said, though I didn't know if it was. I didn't know what to make of him. I felt a peculiar jumbled excitement.

In the weeks and months that followed I waited to see if it would emerge again—this helpless half-formed Michael—but it never did, and mainly I was relieved. I did not want to think about his eyes, which had peered at me in the cafe, soft and almost frightened. It was this moment that kept coming back to me later, despite myself, the way he had looked at me, and each time I remembered it I felt a piercing tenderness, a wanting to soothe and surround; and nestled alongside it, indistinguishable almost, a bolt of fear.

It was nearly six months before I met his mother. She lived in a 1970s apartment set high above a northern beach and framed by the brilliant blues and reds of jacaranda and flame trees.

'She's only invited us to show off the view,' said Michael as we made our way into the living room the first time I visited. He said it loud enough for her to hear, teasing. She was standing on the wide tiled balcony from which she had waved as we got out of the car, but turned as we came into the room and walked quickly towards us.

'Just wait and see,' he said, raising his eyebrows as if this was an old joke, 'we won't hear from her again until this time next year. Mother, Jessica; Jessica, my mother, Sonia.'

She made a show of ignoring him and kissed me, European style, left, right, left.

'My rude son has brought home a beautiful woman for me to meet. I have been trying to get him here for months.'

She was taller than me, and smelled of perfume.

'Michael, what about a gin and tonic for Jessica and I?' She turned to me. 'Gin and tonic?'

I nodded, unable to match her smile. She turned back swiftly to Michael. 'Hello darling darling.' She seized his cheeks between her finger tips, pinched them, almost in parody, smiling fiercely, then moved away again as quickly, back out on to the balcony.

'Darling darling yourself. Ouch.' Michael rubbed his cheeks, pulled a face at me. But he followed her out to where she stood looking towards the ocean, put his arms around her shoulders from behind, leaned his head for a moment on one shoulder. I saw her hands rise briefly to his forearms, locked loosely around her neck, then he spiralled back inside to a heavy wooden cabinet from which he produced glasses, ice in a bucket, gin in a decanter. I sat down on one of the upholstered chairs. After a moment Sonia turned and joined us inside. 'It's chilly,' she said, standing near the doorway, rubbing her arms. 'Michael could you fetch me my wrap?'

'It's there,' he gestured to the chair beside mine, 'on the chair. Jess? Could you?' And I rose and carried it across the room to her. Our eyes barely met as she took it. 'What a lovely name. Jessica. Thank-you Michael.' She inclined her head as she took the drink from him. There was hardly any accent—she had gone to school in Switzerland after the war—except when she said his name. Mikhael. Against hers, my pronunciation sounded flat and nasal. I felt large and unkempt. I disliked her intensely.

'I've been trying to get you here for months,' she continued, speaking to Michael, but smiling slightly at me, raising her glass a little as Michael handed me mine.

This is one of the things we argued about afterwards, that at her apartment and then later when she took us out to dinner (her shout, she insisted) he always gave her drink to her first, before mine. Opened her car door but not mine. (I was relegated to the back.)

'But you hate all that stuff. You wouldn't let me open your door,' he protested, jaw clenched.

'That's not what I mean.'

'If I'd known you were that easy to please. Fine, I'll open doors for you. Is that what you want?'

'Of course not.'

'She's my mother for god's sake. She's an older woman. She's of a different generation. What do you expect?'

'Nothing.'

'Here we go.'

'Here we go what? What's that supposed to mean?'

'Forget it.'

We ate at a small restaurant down the road where the waiters knew Sonia by name and ushered us to a table in the window, and where she ordered, unbidden, half a dozen fresh oysters for each of us to begin with. I had never eaten an oyster, not raw, and now there were six lying exposed and glistening on the plate before me. Embryonic. Obscene. I forced myself to put one in my mouth. I doused it in lemon first, and let it rest a moment on my tongue. But I could not swallow. I knew I would gag. I spat it, under Sonia's concerned gaze, into my napkin and pushed my plate across to

Michael, who shared the rest with his mother.

I knew I had failed. I knew that Sonia would find me lacking. But what I thought later, after the silent drive home, after we had fought and then fucked, as I lay quietly in bed beside Michael, was that the oysters reminded me somehow of him. That day in the cafe when I had told him to go away. The way he had looked at me. His moist defenceless eyes. I couldn't get the feel of the oyster out of my mouth, nesting wetly on my tongue, waiting to be swallowed.

It wasn't that our sex was bad. Far from it. That is what I would have told the psychiatrist in Darlinghurst had I gone back later and had we talked about any of this. At first we were mesmerised. Gloating. In sex, Michael lost his primness and became natural, inquisitive. And I—what did I become? I don't know, I didn't think. I stopped thinking.

It is hard to imagine that now, when all I can remember is baulking and weariness and the sheer effort of rising through my own resistance.

But he moved me. The hollow of his neck, the high collar bones. The muttering in his sleep, curled around himself, away from me. For all the running and the leaping into the sea his shoulders were still small and rounded, like a girl's. When he relaxed they curved inwards, like mine. He had the pointed, pigeon chest of severe asthmatics, children who struggled for breath.

In bed, another night, Michael told me about the dark pan- icked drives to the children's hospital. Him gasping, his mother gripping him tightly by the upper arm, making marks. Just relax, she would tell him fiercely, sit up straight, breathe. Once or twice it was the ambulance, the oxygen mask. Sonia beside him, giving instructions to the ambulance men. She was always right, he said. Even the ambulance men deferred to her.

It had started after his father died. 'Heart surgeon. Heart attack,' he told me. Sometimes at night, alone in his bedroom, he could stop it happening. This is what he believed. If he was careful, vigilant, he could sense sometimes the first hint of breathlessness, of contraction, a whisper in the lungs. If he sat up quietly, his back against the wall by the bed and felt his way into his body, through the teeming fuzz in his chest, he could relax his lungs, soften the constriction the doctors had shown him in the pamphlets on asthma. In through the nose, out through his pursed lips. Slowly. Like blowing out a candle. If he could just get it in time, he could settle it. He didn't tell his mother. She would put on that sharp tight face, and then it would be the hospital. He worked out that fear was contagious. His mother's fear was contagious. He learned to travel to the centre of his fear and calm it. He learned to put it to sleep. He told me this story, in a puzzled, faraway voice, as if this child no longer made sense to him. This body traveller. 'I must have done it for years,' he said, sitting up now, in bed, shaking his head. 'And then I grew out of it. Just like that.' He snapped his fingers. 'And things went back to normal.'

When he told me this, a deep private thing that even he did not understand, my love for him, what I called my love for him, this thick red feeling, rose up and tightened my own chest.

I examine these memories now from a procedural forensic distance.

Early summer, Michael's hip bones protruding, pale, above his Speedos, on the sand at Bondi. 'I don't get this lying down thing,' he complains. He has borrowed my sunglasses, and tilts them back now, and watches as I smear sun block on my arms, legs, shoulders, chest.

'Can you do my back?' I hand him the bottle.

He is meticulous, lifting the straps of my bathers, and rubbing the skin beneath them. 'Have you any idea what's in this stuff? It's poison.' Even without lotion, he will darken to gold then deep brown. My face will get hot and pink and my calves will break out in a rash.

'Look at you,' he says, squatting back on his heels, shaking his head. 'You should be sitting under a parasol. In the shade. Eating sweetmeats, for god's sake.'

'Like a big, fat, pale mushroom—'

'I love your pale skin.' (That is when he said it.) 'I love your large white breasts. I love all the things about you that you hate.'

'Well you probably didn't grow up with your dad telling you to pull your tummy in,' I said, careful not to show my surprise. 'Maybe I could hire you. You could come everywhere with me. Like a motivational tape. Maybe you could be my affirmation.'

'Maybe I could be your husband.'

I remember him saying that. And that brief, startled moment when our eyes met, before I laughed and looked away. And now I don't even know if I said anything. I must have answered. I must have said yes, for we were married not long after. What I remember is the ocean. The first swim of the season. How the coldness exploded around me as I dived deeper and deeper, feeling the waves burst into foam above me.

I reach the campsite well before dark. An uneven clearing a little distance from the track, with a dozen or so tents rising like hummocks beneath the trees. A dirt road leads into the site from the other side, and a group of four wheel drives is parked around the largest stand of gums. A couple of men, dads, are down there tending a fire, and kids, five or six of them, are zig-zagging around them. Already I can smell sausages. I stop before I reach the campers, feeling exposed, uncomfortable at the thought of being among them. Having to talk to strangers, find the rhythm of easy chat, maintain eye contact. There is a sign telling campers to take their litter with them, to light fires only in the barbecues provided, to camp in the numbered sites. I don't want to camp in a numbered site. But nor do I want to camp alone in the bush. On the side of the path near where I am standing is a smaller clearing, half screened from the main site by bushes. I walk over and take off my pack and stand, experimentally, in the place where my tent might go if I pitched it here. If I were to pitch it here. Subjunctive. Provisional. For a moment I feel light-headed. Not dizzy but disconnected, as if the force in my body has risen like steam towards my head, prickling my scalp, sending thoughts or scraps of thoughts out on their own into the cooling air.

I think suddenly of Steff, standing with her back against my door before I left, her large smooth arms folded in front of her. 'You ought to be ashamed of yourself.' She has pulled her voice in, so as not to be heard by anyone passing.

Squat. I say the word, a neutral command, without heat. I lower myself without desire or grace on to my haunches, unconvinced, going through the motions. Ground yourself, says Anna, placid, precise. Squat down, allow yourself to feel your relationship to the earth. Small twigs, mottled and smooth, lie in among fallen gum leaves and thready native grasses. I reach first for those that are closest, gather them in a small pile between my knees. I test one by bending it; it snaps dryly between my fingers. Then, feet still planted in the same position, I reach further out, sweeping from right to left, left to right, feeling the stretch in my thighs and calves, until I have collected a dozen or so twigs within arm's length. Before I stand I place the palms of both hands flat on the ground before me, allow my arms to take some of my weight, then straighten slowly.

I unroll my tent where I am. Place it carefully with the entrance facing in the direction of the other tents—I want to be able to see them—then angle it away a little for privacy. Pull the back of the tent in against the bushes, then out a fraction. It is easy to put up, even alone, and surprisingly satisfying. It is a long time since I have camped. The man in the shop showed me how to assemble the flexible poles and then feed them through the tabs along the sides and top of the tent and into the slots at the bottom. The tension forces the poles upwards and the tent rises. A small green pod in the bush. I push the pegs part way in with my heels and then bang them in further with a lump of wood, leaving a small pile to one side. A moment of concern with the fly-sheet; I put the entrance at the wrong end, facing the bushes. Stuffed it. Shh. Look, it's easy. Just turn it around. See? Eight more pegs. A couple won't go in all the way. I move one, and make do with the other. 'Well done,' says Anna. I put my pack inside, and my sleeping bag; sit for a moment in the filtered light, then climb out and move off into the trees in search of kindling.

When I get back, someone is standing next to my tent. A man. At first I think he is trying to steal it, and I put down my sticks and wait in the bushes, heart pounding, too afraid to move. Then I see the car, the emblem on the side, and I realise that he is a ranger.

'Hey.' My voice sounds small and irresolute.

He looks up, straightens. 'Sorry. You're not allowed to camp here. Campsite's over there.'

He is not unkind. Tall. Younger than I had thought. He waits until I reach him.

'Campsite's over there,' he repeats, gesturing with his head.

'I know,' I say, following his look. Flashes of bright nylon through the trees. 'There's other people there.'

He is standing, looking down at the pile of pegs outside the door of my tent, the green nylon rippling slightly in the breeze. We both look at the pegs and I kick a stray one with my toe, edging it towards the others. Good peg.

'You travelling with anyone?' he says at last.

I don't answer. I divide him into two people. The one who, hearing I am alone, will soften, console. Protect. And the other, who will leave, and return at night when it is dark. It is not being raped that scares me. It is not even being killed. It is the fear before I die.

After a while he says, 'You better move it back then, away from the road. Otherwise everyone coming down'll see you.'

'It's only for the night,' I say, not looking up, in case he changes his mind. 'I'll be up first thing.'

'Still,' he says. 'Better move it back, or you'll get me into trouble.'

I nod vigorously, thank him, make myself look at him.

It is empty when he goes. The air feels thin. As if there is too much space behind me, and nothing to lean into. For a moment I think I will finish dismantling the tent and go across to the main campsite from where I can make out voices, a burst of laughter, the smell of dinner. I feel the rush of the wanting, the need to belong—

to the families, the ranger, I am not even sure. How the wanting blots out the empty space around me; how this is part of its function, the function of desire; and I close my eyes, as Anna has taught me, and feel how it is in my body. The wanting flares, a billowing ache in my chest—lonely—then subsides. After a moment I pull the tent further back into the bushes, gather the pegs and the lump of wood and start hammering them back in. It is nearing darkness when I finish. Inside the tent I undo my backpack, pull out my polar-fleece jumper and torch, lay out my blue foam mat.

A little way from the tent is a circle of rocks and some blackened wood. Someone has camped here already. Perhaps I saw the fireplace before I decided to stop here, noticed without noticing. Perhaps this is why I chose it. The sticks are dry, like the ground, and brittle. I have to go back inside the tent for the newspaper, which is tucked down the side of the pack. I take four sheets, tear them in half, crumple each half, not too tightly, and pile them in the rock circle. Then the sticks, smallest first, a tepee.

'That won't work,' says Michael's voice. 'It'll fall apart. Let me do it.'

And for a moment I let him, reach out to dismantle and start again. Stop myself. Stay still. What is the feeling, says Anna. It is failure. I take the longer, thicker sticks and continue the pattern, propping the ends against the rocks to make them secure. If it fails I will cook soup on the gas ring. From the main campsite I hear a child's voice raised in outrage. Mu-um! The matches are in my pocket, their green, waxy heads hard to strike but waterproof. I cup my hand against the breeze and put the flame to the edge of one of the paper balls, and the dark glow races up the newsprint like air into a lung, catching first the other balls, and then the tiniest of the wood splinters. Michael is right, nearly right. As the paper flares then subsides, the kindling collapses into the centre. I have to put my cheek against the soil, blow gently through my pursed lips—a soft, good wind—to breathe the life back into the fire, give it the force it needs to hold.

I sleep fitfully, dreaming lists and unfinished conversations (a small bird) but always submerged, never quite breaking the surface. In the morning a dull light seeps through the nylon, and beyond the mosquito mesh I see the sky congested with low cloud and, at ground level, a magpie pacing the perimeter of last night's fire.

My clothes smell of wood smoke. I pull them back on over my T-shirt and knickers, squeeze toothpaste on my brush, unpack my hand-towel, unzip the door. Feel outside for my boots, then the water bottle. The main campsite seems closer than it did last night, beginning to wake. I walk around the back of the tents. Some kids are already up and tripping over guy ropes. Resigned threats from parents: if you can't be good/ be quiet/ grow up we'll have to go straight home. There is a tap beside the toilet block. I piss quickly (should have gone behind the tent, flies already circling the drop dunny) then clean my teeth and face, fill up the bottle. Back to the tent, which is still moist from dew. I pull out the pegs, drag my gear from inside, roll up my mat and sleeping bag, push them to the bottom of the pack so that if the ranger comes he will see that I am on my way, that I heeded him, but leave the tent up to dry while I boil water for tea.

Tina has raided the kitchen for me. Tiny hospitality packs of honey and marmalade, silver-wrapped butter pats, the loaf of sliced sourdough. I eat the bread untoasted, from my hand, on a tree stump, two slices with honey, then Viv's second apple, another cup of tea. It doesn't take long to pack the tent up. I strap it to the bottom of the pack, leave it leaning against the stump while I go back to rinse my cup, piss again (body still too careful, watchful, for shitting) and put my apple cores, yesterday's and this morning's, in the bin where they won't spread seeds through the bush and upset the natural equilibrium, or Hil. The pack feels familiar on my shoulders, weighted and not quite comfortable, my skin resisting the pressure. But my back is covered. I put my hat on, feeling complete. Closer to complete.

I move away from the campsite slowly and realise, as I start along the dirt road that leads to the track, that I am looking for the ranger's car. Too early, of course, he probably won't be back until evening. It occurs to me that he is the last person I have spoken to.

'I have to go away for a week or so,' said Anna. 'My mother had a fall. I'm afraid we'll have to cancel next week's appointments.'

I nodded. I looked at her shirt, which stretched across her chest so that I could see the shape of her breasts. I looked away.

'How has your week been, Jess?'

'Okay.' Silence. 'I don't feel much like talking today.'

'Is there something else you would like to do?'

'Not really.'

'Is there anything you want from me?' Silence. 'Is there anything you would like me to do?'

'I don't think so. No.'

It is getting hot, the early moisture thinned and rising. I adjust my hat, thinking that I should have got one with a broader brim. Now that he is gone, well and truly, not coming back, I allow myself to think about the ranger. I think first of—or at least the image that precedes the thinking is of—his arm, the crease on the inside of the elbow, and the pale hairs there. Brown and lightly dusted with yellow earth. He stood next to me for a moment before squatting down in front of the tent and the pile of pegs, pulling a partly hidden metallic wrapper from beneath the tent, Kit Kat, perhaps, crumpling it in his hand and then into his pocket, before rising, brushing his arm—or almost, I couldn't be sure—lightly against mine. It was an accident, clearly. He moved the arm, a deft consolidation, closer to his body, then stepped away not so quickly as to make it look intentional, reactive. A calm, practical movement—away nevertheless—but not to be acknowledged or remarked upon.

I feel the touch of the dusty hairs of his arm against mine, a tiny golden pulse that sweeps, now that he is gone and I can release it, into a sudden lurching in my abdomen, a rhythmic throbbing that spreads in rings from a point midway between navel and clitoris, belly and spine. Now that he is gone I allow myself to linger for a moment on how it might have been if he had come back in the night; that hot pulse and the opening of our mouths and those deep unexpected sounds in the dark. I am thirsty again. In a minute I

143

will open the pack, undo the flask, drink. But for now I can only stand still. Caught in the urgency of my body's wanting. And the ache that spreads with it of not having, not being wanted.

'See you then.' Now that he had stepped back, he looked briefly into my eyes. His were not large, but a strikingly dark brown, like Steff's. He turned with efficient grace back to the car and drove away, raising his arm through the open window in a right-angled salute.

As I walk, my legs extending now into a steady even pace, fragments of last night's dreams flutter and bump against my face. Entrusted to my care is a small bird that cannot fly. I must hold it in my cupped hands while I cross a deep lake. As I wade, the water rising steadily around me, I raise my arms above me to protect the bird, but the floor of the lake disappears and then I am underwater. When I reach the other side and open my palms the bird has drowned.

Twice in the morning cars pass me, four wheel drives, presumably from the campground I have just left. The driver of the first raises a hand as he passes but barely slows, leaving the air behind him turbulent with yellow dust. The second slows, then stops ahead of me. A man and a woman, and two children who strain their necks to peer behind them as I approach. The woman leans out of the passenger side window and asks if I need a lift. They are going on to the next town. I say thanks, but I'm okay. When she repeats the offer, I say I'm meeting a friend further up the track. She looks unconvinced, but does not ask why or how such a meeting would take place.

'Do you have plenty of water?' she asks. 'Because we have some.'

I say yes, I'm fine. It is only as they draw away that I remember with a tightened stomach that one of my bottles is already half empty. It is not so much the water—I will have enough—it is that I did not allow myself to hear her offer before I rejected it, to make the choice. And the feeling that, alone, I am not in good company. The clouds are gone. It is only now that I start to think about bushfires.

'Check the newspaper for fire bans,' the man in the camping shop said, 'and call Parks and Wildlife before you leave and check that the trails are open. You should be okay; it's late in the season, but this sort of weather, things can change fast. Don't want to have to worry about hikers in the park if there's likely to be fires.'

That was three days ago, and I haven't checked since. But there were people last night, and other campfires. And that ranger. It is all right. Close your eyes. Take a breath. 'You should have checked,' says Michael. Yes, I should have. Too late for that now. In bushfire seasons there are always stories in the papers about people in their cars getting caught unawares. The fire fighters say to stay in the car. It is the radiant heat that kills you before the flames get near. Stay in your car and wrap a woollen blanket around you. (What if you had a child? You would wrap the blanket around both of you, and wrap yourself around the child. So that whatever happened to you, your child would be protected.) The fire passes in two or three minutes. Stay low on the floor. The windows might burst but the petrol tank probably won't. The fuller the tank, the safer you are. Less vapour. Wait until the fire has passed, then stay by the car or head back for help in the direction from which the fire has come. (But what then, if it were alone, what would the child do then?) Every year someone cannot bear it. Someone jumps from their car and runs into the bush and burns. It occurs to me, that here, where I am, I am relieved of that choice. If the fire comes I will die. No use fighting.

The trees here are tall up against the road and half of the path is still in brindled shade. I walk through the streaks of light and dark, shrug my shoulders beneath the straps of the backpack, concentrate on distributing my weight evenly on both legs, feel my body release the tension.

Dear mummy, writes Lily, *maybe the Nuthing is scared*—

One day when Lily was small, I was standing at the kitchen sink. It was a Saturday. Michael was running or swimming or maybe working. I was staring through the glass, with its skin of salt, and a voice inside my head said: 'Something is wrong.' It was quite clear, and it was not my voice; it sounded to me like a man's voice, but I did not turn or look around because I understood also that the voice was in my own head, and I was suddenly terribly, deeply frightened. I left the washing in the sink and walked into the living room, past the long, glass-topped table that I would not have chosen and the lithograph above it that I did not like. I went outside on to the landing, leaving the door unlocked, and made my way slowly down the stairwell into the lobby and on to the street. I barely noticed the cafe crowds or the crawling weekend traffic as I went across the road. I was so afraid. I felt that there was an enemy inside. I felt that this voice meant me harm.

On the beach it was windy and grey, and the air whipped up sand and salt spray and attached them to my clothes and my skin, my face. I thought: I am in the wrong place; I must get away from here. I must get away from him. I must escape before the bad thing happens. On my way back to the flat, I told the voice inside my head that it was all right, I would go; it might take a while, but I would go. And then I stopped thinking about it. I forgot.

I had become pregnant almost as soon as we were married. I vomited for two months and ate for seven. People asked if I was having twins. Michael called me Mama Buddha and prostrated himself before me on the kitchen floor. I was happy. At first. Once I had stopped feeling sick I felt strong and sexy and unassailable. I walked with my head high as if before a tailwind. We made love most days. Michael said, 'With my body I thee worship.'

The morning we brought Lily back from the hospital—the wonder of her, the mottled wrists, the frantic wrestling with the baby capsule—I placed her in the white bassinet in our room and without a murmur she slept. For a long time Michael and I lay on the bed beside her and listened to her breathing. Then he undressed me. It was slow because at first I didn't want him to see me: my loose belly, my cartoon breasts. I sat up and he undid my shirt and then the massive feeding bra, one embossed panel then the other (twin cuckoos), until suddenly we were shaking with laughter at the size of me, the proportions. Then he said, not looking at my face this time but at my lap (he spoke firmly and kindly, as if to a patient), 'Let me have a look now.'

I lay back and lifted my arse and he pulled off the elasticised mummy pants but not the knickers because I said, 'No, I'm scared, I don't know what's down there any more.' Michael cupped his hand over the cotton buttress of my pubis and said quietly, 'Poor little cunt.'

'Not so little,' I said in a sad voice, but I let him trace soft lazy

147

finger lines around my underpants and after a while I stopped thinking. He eased them off, opened my legs and gazed until at last I said, 'For god's sake tell me the worst. Will I ever play again?'

Michael looked up at me then and smiled. I smiled right back, and we stayed there grinning at each other like fools while beside us our child breathed in and out, in and out; as if she had been made for it. After a time Michael took his thumb and pressed it softly against the swollen outer lips of my poor cunt, up and down; and then softly against the poor bruised inner lips; here and there; here, there. It didn't hurt at all.

I'm not sure when it all changed. Weeks, maybe months. And I no longer felt godlike, I felt plain and fat and stupid. Michael stopped calling me Mama Buddha. He tried to make me go running and bought low-fat yoghurt. Sometimes I caught him watching me with an odd blank expression. When he was at work I sat on the couch while Lily slept, and rocked back and forth and ate Tim Tams. I was heavy and tired. I moved slowly as if underwater.

When I got back to the flat, that day, Michael was standing stiffly in the doorway, Lily mewing sleepily in his arms. 'The door was left open,' he said in a tight voice. I looked at him and I saw how the colour drained from the skin around his lips when he was angry. I noted his use of the passive voice, how it obliterated the doer, leaving only the done to. I thought how pointless it all was. I heard my voice flat and unresponsive. 'I was only gone five minutes.' Lily was awake now, her face red and puckered, preparing to cry. 'You should have left her sleeping,' I said. 'She hasn't had enough sleep.'

I took her from him then, back into her bedroom, and lay her on the change table on one of her fine muslin sheets, rewrapped her the way the visiting nurse had shown me; pulling the soft fabric firmly over each shoulder and around each arm to keep her from flailing, then wrapping the long ends of the fabric around and around her small body until she lay there like a moth, blinking up at me with her dark eyes. Then I put her quietly on her back in the cot and left the room, as the nurse had taught me, without looking back.

A couple of days later I went to see my doctor, the doctor Michael had found for me. He listened while I talked and then he wrote me a script for antidepressants. I can't say I felt they made much difference, although Michael said they seemed to be working and I probably worried less. But I still didn't like to be alone with her. I was afraid I would damage her.

Coming up now over a small rise, I am disturbed suddenly by a rectangular pellet of sound. It takes me a moment to realise it is my phone. There is a message. I take off my pack and unzip the front pocket. My call directory tells me that someone phoned half an hour ago. I must have been out of range. I don't recognise the number.

In time, it became easier. I learned to think of myself as someone more sensible, someone with a child. I joined a mothers' group and started swimming and cooked meals for when Michael came home. I drank occasionally and not to excess and smoked one or two ciga-rettes a night, that was all. Sometimes I caught a glimpse of myself unexpectedly in a shop front and wondered at the woman reflected back, soft-fleshed, mousy haired, indistinct. Sometimes it was hard to believe I was the same person (the life I had before unharnessed), and sometimes, in the supermarket for instance, or once in a lift, I got a sudden lurching feeling as if the world had slipped and I was falling, and I grabbed Lily's pusher to steady myself. But most of the time things were fine. Pretty good. Once a week we got in a babysitter and Michael and I would go out to dinner or to see a film. Sometimes we had friends around and sometimes Michael talked to me about the work he was doing. More than once he said that I was good for him. When he was home, he played with Lily or walked her to the beach and she waddled after him, face alight, while I sat on the porch or went inside and did the dishes, and thought that I must be lucky, that I must have done something right, although I stopped wanting sex. I didn't want him inside me.

It is odd now to wonder how I managed to lose so much of myself. Sloughed off layer by unremarkable layer. First, the artifice (the bleached hair, the jaunty sunnies), then the attitudes: the sly jokes, the cocked eyebrow, the occasional recklessness; and eventually what you might call the spirit, a certain blitheness.

Anna did not return for nearly two weeks. Twelve days. I told myself that it was the same as always, a period of days that must be traversed. I told myself it was only two hours. I told myself she must not have had sisters or brothers, or they would have looked after the mother instead. The glands in my throat swelled up. I put a note on my door. Do not disturb. That afternoon Steff delivered a letter with my lunch on a tray, propped up so that I could not miss it, and left (stalked out, I thought) without speaking. It was from Michael. On the back of the envelope he had written in large letters, 'Please read. It's about Lily'. Inside was a school newsletter and timetable. School starts at nine and ends at three-thirty but for the first fortnight the new children finish at one p.m. I know the school. It is the one Michael and I visited last year. It is the closest to home, but it seemed quite nice, we agreed later—informal, no uniform. In the principal's office with its open door I felt myself start to soften. Passing children looked in and some waved. The principal, a tall woman with big hands and sensible trousers in a stretchy fabric, seemed patient and practical. She too had been an only child, she said, nodding at Lily, who was fidgeting on my knee, and she remembered how exciting it was starting school and meeting so many new friends.

'I like being an only,' said Lily. 'Because then I can be the boss.' And the adults all laughed.

'You'll do fine,' the principal told her as we left, and Michael and I caught each other's eyes and nodded.

Even so, by the time we got home I was blank with fatigue, a white shutter that descended as I climbed into the car, and through which I could barely decipher images or sound. I asked Michael to drop me at home on the way to Lily's crèche, ignoring her wails and his sharp sigh. Inside I felt my way to Lily's room and her small wooden bed, her pink and white quilt. I woke, still curled on my side, hours later, as if drugged.

My phone rings.

'Jessica,' says a voice, or at least that's what I think it says, and then cuts out. The sound is too distorted for me to tell even if the caller was male or female. I am irritated, first at the caller and then at myself (my curiosity) I check the number. It is the same as earlier today.

The timetable Michael had sent me was full of subjects I

could not understand. Acronyms. LOTE. DEAR. Monday assembly at nine-fifteen. Recess at eleven, lunch at one. I pinned it up on the wall above my bed then took it down ten minutes later, oppressed by the information, the segmentation, the passing of each day.

Even alone, time now tracks me down. Playtime, lunchtime. Who will she play with?

Anna was back the next Tuesday. By eleven-thirty I was edgy, unable to lie still, unable to concentrate. Irritable. I went to the toilet three times, walked into the door the third time, leaving a red mark right in the middle of my forehead. Shit. I left my room at two minutes past eleven and made my way down to the beige room, which was shut. A moment of panic. She had come and gone. Check the hall clock. Three minutes past. I knocked at the door. 'Come in, Jess.'

She was seated. Resting back in one of the green Ikea chairs. So there was nothing to do but go in: don't smile; traverse the room; put my bag down. Why a bag? Why bring a bag? Sit.

'How are you Jess?'

Silence. How am I? She sat quietly in her chair, hands resting in her lap, waiting for my response. I felt my eyes start darting around the room, bookshelf, ceiling. I tried to bring them back to her, to find in my body the repose she so clearly had in hers. I tried to find a feeling that came from inside, not just this raw prowling certainty of being looked at.

Finally, in a tight trying-not-to-sound-tight little voice, I said, 'I hate it when you ask that question. I never know what to say.' Now I could look at her. The ball, I thought, is in your court. Anna didn't change her expression.

'Is there something you'd like me to do instead?' she said.

'Pardon?' A quick surge of panic.

'Is there something else you would like me to do or say?'

Again my eyes started their flickering around the room, her chair, the space above her head.

'I just feel exposed, I feel as if you're staring at me.'

'You don't like it when I look at you?'

'No.'

'You could ask me not to.'

'We can hardly have a whole session without you looking at me.' Terse.

'You could cover your eyes,' she said, unperturbed, putting her hand, visor-like to her forehead, 'like this.'

For a moment I felt like laughing. It was ridiculous. Childish. 'No thanks.' An exhalation. A snort.

'Why not?'

'Because I'd feel—silly,' I said at last.

'What would you like to do in that case?' She glanced at the clock. 'We have, what, fifty minutes to go. Is there something you would like to do with that time?'

I could feel it now. A slow surge deep in my belly. My skin beginning to prickle.

'I just feel very exposed,' I said, talking quickly now, trying to keep the feeling down, bat it away, get it off me. Get her off me. 'I mean it's silly, I know, weird, that I would feel that way, but it's just that sometimes in here I feel like an insect—under a microscope.'

I stopped, waiting for her to speak. She kept looking at me, silent, and eventually said carefully, 'I am aware,' and paused—annoyed, I thought, she sounds annoyed—'that I have made several suggestions and none have been acceptable to you. I notice that you are agitated. Irritable. But that you—'

'I just don't like you asking me all these questions,' I said, petulant, a child.

'Would you like me to ask you something else?'

'No.'

'Would you like me to be quiet?' She paused and when she spoke again her voice was gentler. 'I can do that, you know. Or I can do something else. I just don't know what it is that you want.'

Eventually I said, 'I don't want you to be quiet, either.' I sounded like a child. I heard myself, but I couldn't stop. I laughed, a nervous snort; trapped in this stupid, stupid conversation. 'It's ludicrous, I know.' Another snort. An appeal.

'I find it interesting,' she said. 'You don't like where the conversation is going, and then what?'

'What do you mean?'

'What happens when you don't like something? What do you do with that?'

And I was stuck again. Trapped. Seconds passed. 'I can't—just sit here—and be—looked at,' I said finally, a compressed whisper. 'I feel as if you're judging me.'

'Would you like to check that feeling out with me?' she asked, conversationally. 'Or do you just assume that to be true?'

'What? Oh no, I don't, not at all. I'm sure it's not true. At least, I don't know, maybe it is. I just, I just—' I trailed off again, abject, miserable. 'Shit. Shit. Shit.' As I spoke, I shook my left arm, sharply. Shit. Shit. Shit. Anna looked at me, looked at my arm.

'There's the objection,' she said, as if she had been waiting. There's the bus. 'You might shake your arm again, Jess.' More a requirement than a request. My arm was lying in my lap now, restless, reluctant, prickles of black dancing beneath the skin. I lifted it a fraction, then dropped it. My body sagged forwards. I shook my head. No.

'What is happening, Jess?'

I was slumped over, holding my arms around my thighs. 'Nothing.'

'Doesn't look like nothing. Feel how you have collapsed.'

I pushed myself back to sitting, trying to be normal, invisible. Upright. Immediately my left hand started tingling again. I shook it again, once, helplessly, near tears, trying to flick away this feeling, this black feeling under my skin. Then I took it swiftly, almost roughly, with my right hand, held it in my lap.

'See how you try to check the impulse,' Anna said, quietly, interested but detached. 'Notice that you try to block the feeling.'

I was shaking my head now, like a metronome, I thought. Tick. Tick. Can't stop. Shaking my head, holding my hand, biting my lip. All the time looking at her, willing her to put an end to it.

'Try saying it then,' she said after a moment.

'Saying what?' I became still.

'Shit.'

'No.' A whisper.

'No, then. Say "no".'

I shook my head. I kept looking at her, silently, brought my knees up to my chest, wrapped my arms around them.

'I can't.' I dropped my eyes. A wave of tiredness washed over me.

'Jess. Come back.' There was a slight, pleasant lilt at the end of her sentence, a request. 'Jess, bring your eyes back to mine.'

I closed my eyes, lowered my head to my knees. Drifted.

See. A tiny little thought curled in a shell on the sea floor. Now look what you made me do.

Sometimes when my daughter reaches up to kiss me, I think she does not quite look at me, that her eyes dim slightly, barely discernible, as they meet mine, though her smile is the same, bright and quick, as she steps away and takes Michael's hand. I used to watch them as they walked together up the concrete steps that led to the street and then to crèche. Once they had started I could not turn away. I had to watch until all of her was gone, even her ankles and her feet in their small red shoes. But I thought that it was all right. I think that she is all right. I told everyone what a great dad Michael was. I joked that I'd married a SNAG, that he was the one she ran to if she had hurt herself. (Though I was the one, I reminded myself, who picked her up at the end of the day and read her stories and gave her butterfly kisses.) Sometimes I was out when they left in the morning, at the newsagent or on a walk or anywhere away from the house. I took my time getting home and I came around the back way, where there was no chance of glimpsing them unexpectedly as they climbed into the car or pulled away. Some mornings I stayed in bed, feigning sleep until I heard the door close and had to race for the bus, hair wet, toast in a plastic bag.

'They say at crèche that it's better if you tell the children when you're going,' Michael said one morning, 'and that you'll be back. They've done research. It makes it easier.'

'Who for?' I said, and wished I hadn't.

Michael thought that if he backed it up with research I might listen. And I might. I did. I heard him. 'I hear you,' I said lightly, the second or third time he told me. 'I hear you. You are heard. Is that right? Is that what I'm meant to say?'

He was silent and shrugged and turned away, scooped up her school bag. 'Lil,' he called, 'time to go. Say goodbye to Mummy.'

It makes me laugh though, the things she comes home with. 'You're hurting my feelings,' she berates me (bedtime perhaps, or bathtime, or maybe I have refused her an ice-cream). 'I don't like that.'

Things I would never have dreamed of saying. Still don't. Things I would not even have known how to think. Feelings. 'What feelings?' I say, teasing. 'Which of those feelings of yours am I hurting?'

'All of them,' she says sternly. 'Especially my angry ones.'

My blister is hurting, a deep ache in the ball of my foot, all the more insistent for the relief over lunch. I have been trying not to think about it, but I realise now that the anticipation and then the dark spreading pain are inescapable. I see them in the flame tones of flowers, in the shapes of shadows on the road. Resistance, pain, momentary relief. A morass of feeling. So that the treading into it feels like a punishment, a personal cruelty inflicted by my brain on my foot (you must walk) and then spreading back up from the foot, which now seems enormous, misshapen, through the rest of my body and back at last to my thoughts (you are cruel; you cannot love). I think about stopping. I think about taking a needle (I have one, I am sure, in the first aid kit) and plunging it into the sole of my foot, opening the tender pool, relieving the pressure. But it is too deep, the pain is too deep, and then there is the raw wound and the risk of infection. I must keep walking. (You cannot love.) I must walk.

All afternoon after the session with Anna I paced. Not outside, I couldn't leave the building, nor sit nor read nor converse. All afternoon I prowled the corridors and stairs and any room that was empty. In the dining room I stalked around the tables, set and waiting for dinner, barely seeing, feeling only the jolt of my heels on the lino. It was bright outside, still daylight, but the windows transmitted as blanks, reflecting only inward, and my feet in their socks were awkward helpless claws.

Late in the afternoon as I came down the main stairs into the entrance lobby I caught sight of her, suddenly and unaccountably, across the corridor, through the open door of the sitting room. She was leaving her room, the one where she saw her private clients, turning to pull the door behind her, her day's work done. She looked small at this distance and out of place, one shoulder hitched to keep her bag from slipping: clumsy, unreal. A couple of seconds and she walked out of the frame, heading I supposed for the back exit, the rear car park, her small green Toyota. I stood immobilised on the bottom step, out of time, and after a while noticed my hands gripping the wooden railing. How could I not have known she was still here?

At the last instant I released the banister, sprinted across the sitting room, past the room she had just left, down the hallway to the back door. Even before I got there I saw through the glass panes that she was gone, the car park empty, but I ran anyway, feet scattering the quartz gravel, down the driveway in great shuddering bounds to the entrance, the concrete pillars and the road, which was empty.

In my room I sat at last cross-legged on the bed. I held the pillow to my chest and rocked back and forth, back and forth. I wanted to cry or to shout. I wanted to shout into her face. I wanted to hurt her. 'I hate you,' I moaned, 'I hate you,' but my voice sounded stringy and vague; it could not find the feeling. I started to make sounds, a thick ugly creaking, un-oiled, unhinged. Sounds I had never made before. I sounded like a cow, like a person shitting, like something stuck. I held my pillow against my mouth, pushed my face into it. Rock and moan. In the end, there was nothing but the sound. No more thoughts or ideas or comparisons. Just a droning in my chest and neck and sinuses. In the end, the sound swallowed me, and after a while I felt calmer.

IV

On my fifth birthday we went on a picnic in the mountains, my mother and my father and I. My mother cut sandwiches, vegemite and lettuce, corned beef and chutney, and filled the thermos with hot tea. We put cherry cake, tin cups, condensed milk and apples into the basket. Stuart drove. Once we were out of the city and on to the main road running west to the mountains, we began to sing. This old man, he played one. The owl and the pussycat went to sea. Knick knack paddywack. 'Fare thee well for I must leave thee,' sang Stuart in his light, sweet voice, and my mother joined in, 'Do not let this parting grieve thee; just remember that the best of friends must part, must part.'

When we got to the mountains, to the place my parents called the mountains, Stuart pulled off the bitumen on to a narrow dirt road and we drove into the bush; saplings so close they hit the wind-screen and scraped the sides of the car. My mum and dad used to come here before I was born. I sat in the middle of the back seat and peered between my parents through the windscreen. The path dipped and the car bumped over the rough corrugations, making my teeth clack, then veered up and out and suddenly we were looking at water.

'Here we are,' said Stuart, opening his door and getting out to stretch. 'Our own swimming hole.' It looked like a lake to me.

The pool was below us, and we had to climb down a narrow path through low scratchy bush to reach it. Behind it were high rocks and more scrubby plants. In front of us was a small tawny beach. On a checked rug, my mother unwrapped our sandwiches from waxed paper coloured in pink and blue and green. She called it rainbow paper, and as she took each piece off, I flattened it on the stone beside me into a rectangle or a square.

After we had eaten and taken time to digest, I wriggled into my rubber swimming ring. Stuart and I walked to the other end of the pool and a small rocky outcrop while my mother pulled on her togs behind a tree and then sank into the water, except her head. 'Be careful,' she called. 'Check it, Stuart, for rocks.' Stuart lowered himself into the water, sinking under, then bursting up, spraying water from his hair. 'It's fine, it's fine. She can jump,' he called. 'Swim to me.' The water was the colour of the sand and the cliffs. I could see his face, eyes squinted towards me, his upheld arms, and below that, nothing. I jumped and the water rushed its coolness around me, then I bobbed up, held by my ring, and made see-saw strokes to Stuart. We made our way towards the shore, me hanging on to my dad's kicking legs and laughing, and when we got to the shallows I let go and he stood up and I pulled my ring over my head and crouched low in the water with my lips level to it and imagined that I was a crocodile and that I could swallow the lake and everything in it.

When I stood up I could not see my mother. She was not on the beach, and when I looked back across the water she was not there either. Stuart had not noticed. I asked, or was about to ask, 'Where is she?' when I saw something floating a little way off, not far from the shore. It was big, like a branch, but I knew straight away that it was not a branch. I could see part of her back, with its floral swimsuit, and her long dark hair floating on the top of the water. I was waist deep, and in the icy elongated moment that followed I could neither move nor hear nor speak.

None of it, as I told the psychiatrist that afternoon in Potts Point, was really new to me. As I sat in his corduroy armchair, the day in the mountains repeated the pattern it had always followed. What was surprising was the immediacy, and to realise, if only fleetingly, that despite the familiar plot the day was not quite as I had remembered it after all. It was as if, I now sensed, it had been divided into two—severed, even—and although both parts were known to me, in my mind they were unrelated, two separate histories running side by side, the first, I now realised, taking precedence. I think this must have been where the upset came from, the choking sobs in his darkened front room, feeling the stories suddenly pushed together. And at that point I did think that I would come back and see him again. By the time I was home, though, away from his kindly containing gaze, the two histories seemed to have drifted apart, and I could no longer quite recall why I had been crying.

The second history starts where the first ends. I remember that moment as silent—the moment of my mother's hair—though some slow sound must have seeped out, for Stuart turned as if to look at me, and at the same time my mother raised her head and waved. Stuart waved back and took two or three of his long strides to the shore and I, forgetting I had taken off my rubber ring, started to swim to my mother.

It is strange even at five how clearly things present themselves. There was the panic of course, and the rushing sense of displacement (my hands, which had nothing to hold), but my main recollection is one of embarrassment (my foolishly flailing legs) and then the descent.

Stuart carried me to shore. 'She's all right,' he kept saying as my mother reached us, 'she's all right'. But my mother was not listening.

'What were you thinking, what were you thinking?' she muttered to Stuart, or to me, over and over, as she snatched me from him.

In the psychiatrist's corduroy armchair, I could feel her face very close to mine. Over her shoulder I could see Stuart's mouth opening and closing behind her, everything wrong, because of me. And I felt myself engulfed, suddenly, in rage. I shouted shrilly at my mother to let me go. When she did not I pushed her hard, as hard as my arms would allow, and fell suddenly away.

The next image in this memory chain is of my mother and father fighting. I do not recall the content of the argument, but I have a clear sense of their placement, against a backdrop of pale peeling tree trunks, and me, a little distance away now, drawing with a stick in the dirt. They were not shouting. My mother was speaking fast and low, looking not at my father but at the ground beside him, and my father at one point, quite casually it seemed, reached out and struck the tree trunk nearest to him with his fist. I do not recall any sense of urgency, nor do I remember deciding to run. Nearby, however, was a set of wide dirt steps leading down, and then a narrower set, and then a dirt path to the right with a ruckus of low sharp shrubs on either side, along which I now charged.

Hil says it was not this way at all. She says that the two events—the moment of my mother's hair and the moment on the mountain track—were separated not by minutes but months. That during that hot summer my parents had driven to the mountains several times, and that she, Hil, had even swum with us one day in the same pool, which was at least five kilometres lower down the mountain. 'But Hil,' I insisted, 'it happened on my birthday!'

Hil shrugged. 'What do you want me to say, mate?'

Either way, sitting with my eyes closed in the psychiatrist's room in Potts Point I could recall with an unexpected, almost physical clarity the movement of my body along the narrow green passage and the point at which it altered suddenly and I stopped. In my urgency I had formed no sense of anything beyond the path, of the tall gum trees to my left or the sandstone escarpment rising to my right. Now as I stood I saw two things. I was in a small clearing, or at least a wider section of path. To my right, opening into the rock a little above me, was the mouth of a cave, a dark slab of air. To my left, where there had been trees and shrubs, there was nothing.

In the pulsing silence around me, I could hear only the cicadas and the shuddering of my own breath. I could no longer hear my parents or tell if they were still arguing. I was on the edge of a great cliff. It stretched away in either direction in ribbons of yellow and brown. Far below, further than I could imagine, was green. Had I not stopped when I did I would have gone straight over into nothingness. In the lee of this knowledge, and the great fright that now rumbled through my body, the small strip of sandy soil that separated me from that nothingness seemed to list and tilt in the heat, now wider, now narrower and shrinking. I had the powerful sense that at any moment I would pitch headlong into the abyss, that this time my parents would be unable to save me; and I saw again my mother's dark hair in the water. It was then that my legs buckled beneath me.

For a while I lay there with my cheek pressed hard against the yellow dirt until the rocking subsided and then, without looking back, I crawled on my arms, dragging my heavy blank legs, and pulled myself in this manner up towards the opening of the cave. Inside, the space was wide with a sandy floor and a low roof that sloped down to create a small dim chamber at the rear. I hauled myself as far in as I could, until I had wedged myself safely into the crack. And there I lay and waited for my mother to find me.

When I awoke it was black.

It is not strictly true to say, as people do, that someone wakes from a trance. I did not feel that I was waking, I felt simply that my attention, which had wandered, under the psychiatrist's guidance, into a richly hued daydream, had now returned, leaving me a little startled. As if a wave I had been surfing had dumped me unexpectedly on the beach. I felt oddly bereft, and it was about now that I was briefly consumed by the intense alarming sobs. When I had calmed myself, the psychiatrist said that if I would like to return the following week we could explore the day further. But although I nodded, I felt in truth that I did not want to revisit that emptiness. Besides, I already knew what happened next.

When I awoke, it was morning and someone was saying my name. It was a man; he had a beard and shorts and crouched at the mouth of the cave, calling softly, as if too polite to come in. He had in his hand a walkie talkie, into which he spoke, and which he demonstrated for me as we stepped out of the cave and on to the path. I still have in a folder in my bedroom at home a yellowed newspaper clipping bearing the headline 'Mountain girl lost'. Now, though, as friends and neighbours in Sydney opened their papers to read about my disappearance, we walked, the ranger and I, together along the path, back the way I had run, and the ranger held my hand calmly and firmly.

Some time afterwards, ahead of me on the track, I saw a small group of people and, as I watched, my mother detached herself and started to walk quickly towards me. I recall that she looked to me immensely distant, a small figure dwarfed by trees and sky and that even when she yelped and called my name and I raced and clung to her, I felt a strange sense of dislocation, of slippage, as if during the night, without my knowing it, something had altered. As I walked beside her, retracing our steps along the track towards the car park where we would shortly be met by my father, I held my mother's hand tightly and did not pull away even though with every wordless step the sense of dread was growing. I could not overcome the feeling that I had left something in the cave. That there was less of me now than there had been when I entered; that while I slept some cog or link had come adrift and was now lost, perhaps forever.

It was late afternoon by the time we left the mountains. There had been doctors and television interviews and police. There had been a trip to the hospital and lunch at a tall hotel with red velvet curtains. There had been my mother and father standing in the hotel foyer, his arms wrapped around her. There had been a curly-haired doll with blue glass eyes, and gradually the feeling had dropped away. As we drove back down towards the city, the wind rushed past us and in through the windows in warm gusts that smelled of eucalypt and earth. Stuart strummed the dashboard with his free hand and sang a song, to make me happy, about a man trying to kiss a girl, and when he had finished I laughed and clapped and then my mother began to sing. Her voice was so low and slow that at first it was not like singing.

'True love, true love, don't you lie to me, tell me where did you sleep in the night?'

Stuart joined in. 'In the pines, in the pines,' they sang, 'where the sun never shines.'

Stuart glanced across at my mother and they took it in turns to sing the parts. He was the man and she was the woman. Back and forth. And always the man was trying to find out things about the woman.

'In the pines, in the pines,' sang my mother, 'where the sun never shines.'

When they finished I could not speak. We were all quiet. It was like being on the edge of something. I sat very still and made my breathing soft and tried to hold it all steady, the wind and the hum of the car and my father and my mother.

When we were close to home, my mother began to cry. She pulled herself into a ball in the front seat and rocked from side to side.

'Sweetheart?' said Stuart and reached across and touched her shoulder with his spare hand.

She cried so much her face was red and slippery. Stuart pulled over and hurried around the car to open her door from the outside.

'Steady, steady,' he said, crouching down. She said something into his shoulder, muffled. And he stood and came around to open my door. 'It's okay, Jess, you come with me.'

He held me by the elbow and walked me quickly across the road to a fish and chip shop where he bought me an orange drink and asked to use the phone. When I was back in my seat, my mother turned around and reached back to stroke my cheek. Her face was not quite right. I had never seen her cry.

'It's all right, darling, Mummy's not feeling very well.'

Perhaps Hil is right. Perhaps we went home after that, my mother and father and I, and I slept. And perhaps the days after that continued uneventfully. But that is not how it feels. To me the two memories, the pool and the cave, remain encased forever in the same smooth skin, and they always end the same way.

Before we got to our house, Stuart drove to Hil's. She was waiting at the gate, expecting us. She opened my door and when I climbed out she gave me a bear hug. Then she held me as I leaned in the car window to kiss my mother goodnight. I slept in her bed. The next day I started school, and when I got home my mother had gone.

V

The guy at the outdoor shop tried to talk me out of coming this way.

'Take your time,' he told me. 'There's some wicked country out there, some of the best tracks in the world.'

He was thickset, not tall, with short cropped hair that glinted under the store's fluorescent lights and a tattoo encircling his upper arm, Maori-style.

I said I knew and that perhaps I would try one of them next time. He said there might not be a next time, and although he was smiling, he did not seem happy and his voice sounded almost sharp. On my way out, however, he called after me and told me to keep a look out for the hanging swamp. I said I would, and he made a thumbs-up sign. Now, remembering the conversation, I wonder what I am meant to be looking for. I do not know what a hanging swamp is, or where to find it. I decide I must have missed it, and for a moment wonder whether I should turn back, retrace my steps, looking properly this time. Or maybe I have not yet reached it. Or perhaps in this heat the swamp has dried out and died.

My mother left a letter. It didn't say much but I learned it by heart and Hil, who had moved in with us by then, was forced to read it to me last thing at night for weeks until she got fed up and hid it in the linen closet, where I found it many years later.

The letter said my mother would not write again for a while and that I should not wait for letters, but that she would think of me every day. She did not leave an address. As I got older I became convinced that Hil must know her whereabouts, must even be in contact with her, but no matter how much I probed and cajoled, she would only change the subject or deny it, and after a while, realising that if I pushed too hard she would simply walk away, I stopped asking. All I knew from my mother's letter was that she had gone to live in America, and that there were some things that grown-ups could not easily explain to children, but that one day she was sure we would sit down together and talk about everything.

I knew also, although it wasn't in the letter and I don't remember how I found out, that my mother had gone to live with a man, an American she had met at school where she had been studying sociology. In the playground during recess I would mesmerise myself with precise detailed fantasies, from which the American was excluded, in which my mother was there one day waiting when I walked out of school to take me home.

In class, when the teacher told us to draw a picture of our family, I drew my mother in the kitchen floating above the table. While Stuart and Hil and I sat below, poised over dishes of strange, brightly coloured food, she bobbed along beneath the ceiling, her legs trailing behind her like pond weed.

When people asked, I told them she had drowned. I could describe in great detail the lake in the mountains where she died. How my father and I had pulled her out. And after a while I decided to believe it.

Up ahead the road rises and curves, parched and yellow, made of dirt. In my mind the hanging swamp floats above me, anchored over the sandy track like a pontoon of flat-bottomed clouds, moisture saturating the brilliant green mosses, sunlight catching the droplets as they drip and plash from level to level like tiny glinting waterfalls. If I listen I can almost hear them.

It takes me a while to realise my phone is ringing again. At first I can't quite decipher the sound, then I reach behind me with one arm and twist my elbow to reach it. There is a woman's voice, husky and almost familiar. She doesn't introduce herself.

'Jessica?'

'Yes.' My voice in my ears is plaintive and over-loud.

'I just wanted you to have our address, in case you want to come and visit.' The speaker, who I know that I know, but cannot yet place, doesn't pause. 'You could come any time. There's a spare room—or there's even a flat, downstairs.'

'I'm sorry—'

'I don't mean to be pushy. People are always telling me I'm pushy and I don't mean to be. I just thought you might like…It's very beautiful up here. There's a small boat. You could use it whenever you wanted. It used to be Hugh's but he won't be using it for a while.'

The boy's mother. Hugh's mother. Laura.

'He might not be using it at all. You probably think I'm mad—'

'I don't think you're mad. I just—I don't think you're mad. I'm not sure what my plans are—how's he going?' I add quickly before she can speak again.

'Well of course the doctors are calling it miraculous, at least his GP in town did—Dr Orzasky seemed to think it was all in a day's work, but he has to say that really, doesn't he? Americans. Don't you find Americans very brash? Yes, I thought he was a bit brash, but he helped things along I suppose. No more than you did though, in my opinion.'

'Oh, well I didn't do anything—' I want to tell her that he is not American, he is Canadian, but Laura tumbles on.

'Of course you did. You did! Or at least you helped me. And now it looks as if he's going to be all right. Well nearly all right.' She slows at last. 'Of course we don't know if he'll sing again.' I hear her breathe in slowly. 'He says he doesn't want to sing.' There is a pause. 'Anyway,' she resumes, 'we got home last night, and I thought of you.'

'Laura, did you ring before?'

'Yes, I might have done. I heard you'd left, and I wanted to contact you before, you know…well, anyway.'

'Laura?'

But she has gone.

In the newly gathering silence I pull the pack into a small patch of shade and sit in the dirt on the side of the road, still holding the phone. The conversation with Laura has depleted the charge. Only two notches left. I should turn it off, preserve the power. I finger the button on top of the phone, but in the end I don't press it. I put the phone back into the backpack, and pull myself up to start walking. I leave the phone on just in case. I leave it on in case Anna rings.

By the time I saw my mother again I was fourteen. There was another long letter first, hand-written in blue biro, in which she talked about her 'journey' and 'healing' and about her and Hil growing up on a farm an hour's drive from the nearest town, and their father who drank and their mother who drowned—this was the only part of the letter that I found interesting, the silent father and the dead mother and the two little girls, the one who became my mother and the other who was and always will be Hil.

I asked Hil about it later, in a roundabout sort of way to try and trick her into talking, but she just stood up from the couch where we had been drinking cocoa and brushed her palms brusquely on her jeans and said it was all old history now and that was how it should be, and that was that and it was time she got down to the Dump. I was cross with myself for not thinking it through or remembering that the best way to find out about Hil was to get her talking about someone else.

Three afternoons a week at three o'clock she still walks up the small steep street behind the cottage to the redbrick hall she talked council into turning into a youth club, and stays there until closing time at ten. When I was a kid and still living with Stuart, she used to pick me up from school and we would walk there together hand in hand, and there I would wait until Stuart came and got me. At first I did not want to go. I was scared of the kids, although I did not say so to Hil. For the first few weeks, she tells me, I would not come out from the little glass-fronted office where she paid accounts and organised fundraising and spoke to parole officers and sometimes angry parents. But there was a trampoline and pretty soon there were friends, and besides, there was no choice. These kids were disadvantaged and it was up to Hil to look after them. I couldn't see what all the fuss was about. I was disadvantaged and no one made any fuss about me, least of all Hil.

In her letter, my mother wrote that she had been very unhappy when I was a child, but that this was not my fault and that there had not been a day since that she had not thought of me; that she was coming to Australia next month for a couple of weeks and that she very much hoped I would see her. She did not say she was sorry; not that a letter would have been the place for it.

We met, for reasons I can no longer remember, outside the North Sydney swimming pool where, as it turned out, she had just swum. Her wavy brown hair, longer now, was still wet and there were reddish indents around her eyes where her goggles had been. We were the only two standing there, so it was not hard to find her. She apologised immediately for her dishevelled state and wondered aloud whether she might have been trying to disguise herself, to give herself the advantage of recognising me first. I said it was fine and that I was not sure I would have known her anyway. She looked smaller than I remembered and thinner, and somehow less, although her arms were brown and sinewy. Beside her I felt pale and soft. She spoke with an American accent, which I had not expected. She said she had borrowed a car from a friend and could give me a lift back to Bondi afterwards if I wanted. I told her I was planning on having a swim myself, nodding at my shoulder bag. She laughed a little too fast and made a joke about blood and water that I did not catch, and her hand flitted for a moment towards my forearm, as if to touch, then dropped away. Beyond the pool was the harbour with its bridge and ferries and its hundreds of small white handkerchiefs. My mother looked from me to the water and back, and perhaps there was a flicker then, something deep between us. Her eyes were green. I asked if she was going to see my dad and she said no.

I don't remember much more. We went and sat on a bench from where we could look at the view, and while she watched it I watched her, and tried to make sense of her strange new face, which was creased and beautiful and after a while gave me a headache. As we sat, she lit herself a cigarette, for which she also apologised. She asked after Hil and nodded repeatedly as I told her that she had bought herself a cottage around the corner from Stuart and me, and about the Dump. And my mother kept nodding, like a sharp bright bird, and said of course, she remembered. I didn't know why she had asked, as I was sure that she must know all this. She said, 'Do you think she is happy?' I shrugged and said I supposed so.

'I miss her,' said my mother. 'She thinks I have done the wrong thing.' As she sat, she leaned forwards from her hips as if into a strong wind. She said, 'You must be very angry with me,' and I shrugged again and said I didn't really feel like talking. She nodded. I felt bad for her, but I still didn't want to say anything. After a while she said that she had made a mess of things. Then she said that she was doing a degree in psychology and that Ted, who I supposed must be her husband, was building her a studio in the garden where she could work and that I had a half brother whose name I promptly forgot. Soon after I asked if she could drive me home as I wasn't feeling well.

When we got to Bondi, she parked a little way from the house and got out of the car when I did. I was scared for a moment that she would try to hug me, but instead she held out her hand and we shook. She had warm hands and long useful fingers with short bitten nails. The next day, she rang to see if I wanted to come to Manly with her on the ferry. I said no, that I had homework, and she left me a phone number and asked me to call. Hil said that it might be good for me to spend some time with her. 'She's your mother, mate.' I said I hadn't noticed, and anyway I hadn't seen Hil rushing off to visit her.

'She smokes now, you know,' I said.

'She knows where I am,' said Hil.

I went to bed. I didn't call and when the phone rang I didn't answer it. She wrote when she got back to America, giving me her details and telling me to write or ring any time. She underlined the last two words. I thought about it once or twice but that was all. I found her alarming. As if somebody had taken away the mother I once had, and replaced her with a counterfeit.

Once or twice a week at the nursing home I used to help Viv out with paperwork in the office. I had started updating her filing system, though not officially; she wouldn't have liked that.

'Just bringing you into the new millennium,' I told her.

Viv had been there for thirty-five years, and she still had the details of every resident who had passed through the place filed alphabetically in concertina files above the desk.

'Who's this?' I said one day as I was idling in the office. 'Marjorie Walker. Who's Marjorie Walker?'

'Oh, Marjorie.' Viv paused for a moment, tilted her head. 'She was here in the early eighties, I think. Eighty-two. Eighty-three she died. I think it was March. She had a big funeral up in Willoughby, I think it was. She came from money. Her husband was in copper. Or zinc. Something metally.'

'But she's been dead nearly twenty years.'

'Yes.'

'So why have you got her filed in here next to Mrs Wong from room thirty-three?'

'W. Walker. Wong. No, that can't be right. We've had a Weston. Joyce. And a couple of Wilsons. At least two, there was Reg and his wife. Come here. Give it to me.'

'Viv,' I said after a minute. She was still flicking her way through the file, lips pursed, trying to find the missing Wilsons. 'Why have you got all the living people mixed in with the dead ones?'

'Why not? There's no point changing it all around, it will disrupt my system. I know where everyone is.'

'But couldn't you at least have one new file, with just the people who are here now? I could do it for you if you want. And then when they die, or leave, you could file them with the others.'

'No,' she said briskly, climbing up on the piano stool to put the W file back on its shelf. 'It's fine as it is.'

'Don't you get sick of clambering up and down every time you want a file?'

'Not that I'd noticed.'

But about a week later she stopped me in the corridor on my way back from breakfast. 'All right,' she said. 'You can come in and do a new file for me. And you can tidy up the rest, make sure they're in order. But that's all. I don't want anything messed up or thrown out. Don't go reading anything you shouldn't. All right?'

I started with the A's. Abbot, Allen. Anderson, Rose—take her out and put her in the file of the living, for now at least. The manila folders were mainly taken up with medical records: diagnoses, prognoses, medications, test results. As well as information on each resident's discharge or death. Then there were other bits and pieces that Viv had seen fit to conserve. Christmas cards from relatives thanking Viv and her staff for the work they were doing. Receipts from the man who came to fix the washing machine. Pamphlets from pharmaceutical companies. Cards written in wavering script from long-dead residents.

The names thinned out at the end of the alphabet. A surge of W's. Weston (Joyce), Williams (three of them), Wirth, Wirihana, the two Wilsons, a Watson, two Wongs. Even, I noted, a White. X Y and Z shared a file. Xanthopoulous. Xuerab. Somehow a P had found its way in here with the X's. Parker. Xanthe Parker, her first name, so much more exotic than her second, taking precedence in one of Viv's distracted moments. Xanthe Parker had been dead eight years. I wondered if Viv would know where to find her now. Probably. Eight or nine Y's, a couple of Z's. I flicked along the name markers dividing each file, and stopped at Young. It was habit more than intent that stopped my thumb, a matter of placement; this is where I fit. There were two Youngs. And even though some part of me must have anticipated it, it was with a little startle that I found my name on the second. Jessica Young. I wondered if Viv would call this reading something that I shouldn't.

The file was thick with papers. I glanced quickly at the card in front—name, date of birth, admission date, and then more cards bearing details of my condition and circumstances. Diagnoses, medications, test results (inconclusive). There was an envelope, addressed to Vivienne Elder; something familiar about it. Checking the date on the postmark—two weeks after my illness began—and realising of course that the writing was Hil's. Her chunky long-hand marching across the page, inside as well, two sheets. She doesn't type, won't use a word processor. 'Dear Viv, I know it's been a long time, but I could do with your help again, if you can manage. My niece—'

I stopped reading and folded the letter back into its envelope, following the creases, and buried it back in the file. Moving swiftly, without thought, to the next entry, the other Young. Glancing at the name. Isn't that strange, I thought—that odd lag the mind engineers under pressure—she has the same name as my mother. What a coincidence. And then I realised it was not a coincidence, that of course it was my mother, my mother's file. I didn't know how I knew, no one had told me she was ever here, it just settled on me with a clear certainty. And I realised also—but as if I had always known it, the brain still working backwards—that this was why the place had always seemed familiar. First, in fact, the recognition of the familiarity, and then the other understanding slotting quickly, efficiently into place. Effect and cause. The mind separating now into layers or planes, each operating independently but in unison, each producing or retrieving its own insights or images; the mind's contents unstacked and laid out before me. I had come here when I was little. I remembered the bronze plaque next to the front door. The slack face against the pillow. ('Dear Viv, I could do with your help again.')

'Give your mum a kiss, mate.' Hil.

'That's not my proper mummy.' I am not yet three.

And as quickly as it had opened, the mind closing, reassembling, stacking up. Tightness at the base of my skull; that's the shock.

My hand, I noticed, was shaking. In an envelope stuck to the inside front cover of the file was her card, written in spidery black handwriting that even now I recognised as Viv's. She had been admitted in November, a little over two years before she left for America. Age, 33; the same as me. Underneath, in Viv's truncated notes, I could make out the words 'valium' and 'depression'. I closed the folder.

'Well of course they were there. I thought you would have known.' Viv was in on her way to a meeting. 'You didn't have to read them.'

'Why didn't you tell me?'

'Well, as I say, I thought you knew. And besides, it wasn't up to me.'

Hil was no better. 'We didn't think you'd remember,' she said at last. 'You only came the once.'

'You're not sick, you know, not really,' said Viv one day soon after, as I sat at the roll-top desk, putting stamps on envelopes. Overdue accounts. 'Not any more. You're a bit weak still, that's all. You should get back to Sydney. To your friends. Family.' It was the middle of the afternoon and the sun was slanting through the window on to the couch, where George the cat was asleep, stretched out on the padded floral arm.

'I'm still doing quite a bit of work with Anna,' I said. 'It's odd that Rose's family hasn't paid.'

'You shouldn't really be seeing those accounts,' said Viv, sounding annoyed, as if she had not asked me to sort through them. 'They're private. You're not meant to know who's paid and who hasn't, all the other residents. Anyway, you can still see Anna Greene; nothing to stop you from seeing her. She's got her own practice.'

'Yes, I know.'

I licked the last stamp and stuck it down smoothly with my thumb.

'I wonder,' says Anna, 'if we might do an exercise. Would you like to do an exercise? It's very simple, and quite energising.'

One night after dinner Michael said, 'Someone's trying to sue me.'

Lily was asleep in bed, and we were sitting side by side on the back step of his flat, our flat, listening to the sea rasp against the sand at the other end of the street. I was smoking a cigarette, and we were drinking red wine from tumblers. I was wearing a cardigan over my dress because the weather had started to turn, but the evening was still mild and scented with salt. It was Friday and Lily had just finished her orientation week for her new school, where she would go the next year (where she has gone, I remind myself; where she now *goes*). I was pleased. The teachers were friendly, I'd told Michael, and Lily had decided she would stay there until she was seven or ten. He had laughed, briefly, and we had been sitting in what I took to be an uncomplicated silence. I was relieved—far more than I told Michael, or even myself—that she had taken to it so well, that I had not had to work my way through tears and promises and unnavigable guilt.

I was, if not peaceful, at least satisfied. Michael was working hard and seemed mainly cheerful. We argued less over sex and he no longer talked about wanting a second child. Sometimes I took pills to sleep. In my mind we were treading water. The water felt okay. It didn't feel too bad.

'A woman,' he said.

'A woman is suing you?'

'Threatening to sue. We gave her a general. She says the anaesthetic was inadequate.'

'Meaning what?' I picked up the dictionary lying next to me on the step and started to flick through it, reluctant to give up the evening.

'She's saying she remembers the operation.'

'She's saying she remembers. What was it, a caesarean? What does she remember? Could she hear you?'

Inadequate, I read: not adequate; insufficient. Not capable or competent; lacking.

'She's wasting her time. She wasn't conscious. There was no problem with the anaesthetic. She's got some psychiatrist saying she remembered the surgery under hypnosis.'

'Was the baby okay?'

'The baby was fine. Don't worry about it. It won't come to anything.'

'Inadmissible,' I read aloud. 'Not admissible or allowable. So she's not saying she was conscious. She's saying she remembered things later, but only after she was hypnotised. And what does Roger say? Can't he sort it out?'

'He doesn't need to sort it out. It won't come to anything. Don't worry about it.'

'What does it mean if you're being sued? Is it you, or us, or the hospital? Who's she suing?'

'No one. I just thought I'd tell you. It won't happen.'

But a few days later it was in the papers. Michael brought it in and dropped it on the kitchen table.

'Here we go,' he said.

It was a small story on page four. *Woman sues over birth 'nightmare'*. I read the first few paragraphs. Her name was Andrea. She was thirty-one. She was suing St Mary's hospital, surgeon Roger Ellis and anaesthetist Michael Small. She claimed to have suffered depression and ill health after the birth of her first child. Under hypnosis she had told her psychiatrist she remembered a conversation in the delivery theatre. She said she remembered one of the doctors calling her a whale, saying they would need a forklift to move her. She was suing for compensation for psychological distress, claiming professional misconduct.

'That's not possible, surely, that she could remember things like that?'

'Who knows, there can be some recall. But the hypnosis stuff will never stand up in court.'

'So did anyone say anything? Who called her a whale?'

'No one that I'm aware of.'

'So she's making it up?'

'Imagining it, more like.' He folded the paper. 'I'm late.'

Michael didn't bring it up again. Once or twice I asked, and he said again that it wouldn't go to court, that the woman had no case. I asked him again about hypnosis. Using the woman as an example, did that mean then that, theoretically at least, it would be possible for someone, for that woman, to have taken in information while she was unconscious? To have in her memory things she didn't even know she knew but that could still affect how she behaved or felt? Was that what it meant?

No, said Michael, because the things she said had happened hadn't happened.

But technically, I persisted, would it be possible, technically, for someone to remember in that way?

Michael said no.

All afternoon as I walk thoughts clamber up my throat and get stuck there, making pressure.

A week or so later there was a knock at the door. Lily was playing in the lounge room with a friend from crèche. Michael was at work. I had a headache. I had had it for about three hours. I knew who she was. I had never seen her before but I knew who she was. I stood in the doorway, and said, 'Yes?' I wondered where her baby was. She said, 'You're married to that Dr Small aren't you?'

'Who are you?' I could feel my heart starting to pound. I blocked the doorway with my body.

'I'm not going to hassle you,' she said. 'They're going to pay me out, the hospital. They're going to pay me to keep my mouth shut. And after this I will. I just came to tell you what they said while I was having my baby, your husband and all them other nice men.'

When Michael got home that evening, Lily was excited because I'd let her have crap for dinner. She showed him the plastic toy.

'Great, honey,' he said, and then to me, 'Couldn't you at least have got pizza?'

'Andrea Roberts came around.'

'Honey, Daddy's got to talk to Mummy for a moment,' he said at last. 'Go and get into that bath and I'll come in a minute and wash your hair. What did she say?'

'You tell me. Why didn't you tell me?'

'Because I didn't think it was necessary.'

Christ, she's like a whale. Women this fat shouldn't have kids. That was what one of them said.

Women this fat shouldn't have sex. That was what the other one said. Then there was laughter, and then a third voice cut in, a quieter male voice.

'Well, if she doesn't pull herself together she's going to end up losing her husband.'

That's what she told me. Afterwards she shuffled back up the drive without looking back, and I watched her get into her car, a small brown Corona or something similar, with a child seat in the back.

Michael was as pale as I've ever seen him. Eventually he said, 'I didn't mean it like that.'

Had he laughed, I asked him, had he laughed with the others? Had he laughed when they said she was too fat to have sex?

He said no he hadn't laughed, he didn't think it was funny. But nor did he think it was worth destroying a career over. Two careers. Three.

'She can't breast feed,' I told him, my voice veering upwards.

'She can't make herself hold her baby. She can't even look at him. Her mum's looking after him.'

'You can't say that, Jess; you can't assume that those things are related.'

'I bloody well can,' I told him. 'How come the hospital's settling out of court?'

'Those things would probably have happened anyway for that woman. It happens all the time. Mothers get post-natal depression, you of all people know that. I understand how hard it seems, but it doesn't make sense to get so upset about it.'

'It bloody does,' I said, near tears. 'It does!'

He sighed, and in response my voice rose further, shrill now, almost comic. 'So does that mean you'll leave me now? Will you leave me because I'm fat?'

That startled him. 'Jess. No. What are you saying? Of course not. And you're not. What is this?'

His arms and legs, I noticed as he spoke, seemed only loosely attached to the rest of him and, with his head shaking from side to side, he reminded me of a marionette. I wondered for the first time if he was good at his job. I had always assumed he was; now I didn't know. Not because of what the woman, Andrea, had said, but because I saw now that all the bits of him didn't seem to fit together, as if he had to think about them all the time, keep them in check or decide what to do with them. It must take a lot of effort, I realised, not being angry with me.

And at that moment I wanted to tell him the truth. I wanted to tell him what this was, but I couldn't. So instead I told him what I had forgotten to tell him that day when Lily was small. I told him I was leaving him.

Cause and effect. It was almost funny after all this time to see that I could make a difference. Michael looked like a ten-year-old. He actually looked as if he had been hit, as if I had hit him, although when he spoke it was with his normal talking voice. 'I had an affair,' he said quickly. 'I had an affair with one of the nurses; it's a cliché, it's over, I'm sorry. I'm sorry. Please Jess.'

And then strangely, because even I could see it was not what he meant to do, he gave me a small shy smile. It was the smile that shocked me. It was the smile of someone without a backup plan.

And instead of rage or desire or any of the other things a wife might have felt at that point, what I felt was nothing. Not an empty nothing, not an absence or a stillness or a space between thoughts, but a nothing like a slammed door. Like an axe. I wanted to feel those other feelings; I knew they were probably there. But I could not. And so I said nothing. I left it to him and he said all the things I had wanted him to say: about needing me and never leaving me; about us moving to another place, a proper house; about his childhood and about his father and about his mother, and even (though I stopped listening then) about mine. He said everything and none of it mattered. I was looking at his face and its expression, which I could not name.

When I looked away from him, Lily was standing in the doorway, thoughtful in her towel. And then I couldn't talk any more because my head ached too much, a greenish throbbing that fitted like a skullcap and now seemed to stretch down my neck and shoulders into my kidneys, my buttocks, the backs of my knees. 'I feel like shit,' I told him. 'I'm going to lie down.'

'Can I bring you something?' The doctor again.

I didn't answer. I felt really quite ill. Lying on top of the bedcovers, curled in a ball, I could hear the low square mounds of Michael's words from the bathroom, and after a while Lily's high singing. They sounded a long way away. I woke briefly some time later and Michael's voice was beside me. 'Jess, are you awake?' He sounded small and worried. I tried to sit up but I could not move. There was a dark buzzing sound in my head, and through the buzzing Michael kept saying, 'Jess, wake up.' I tried to answer him but I could not hear my voice and am not sure if I spoke.

The last time I saw my mother was shortly before I met Michael. She wrote and suggested, as she had once or twice before, that she pay for me to come to America to stay with her and meet her family. I don't know why I decided to accept this time. I told myself it would be good to see the States. I even hoped she might send me a round the world ticket, but in the end there was a lot of to-ing and fro-ing over dates and connections and it turned out she was using her husband's frequent flyer points. He was an academic and travelled a lot to deliver papers. They had been saving points for some years, she told me during the brief flurry of phone calls that followed my letter back, hoping I would decide to come.

On the phone she talked fast and a little breathlessly, confirming schedules and itineraries, saying again how pleased she was, checking even on my dietary needs—meat? (yes) dairy? (yes)—and

I was reminded again of a bright quick bird, one whose metabolism required that it only ever alight briefly before moving on.

She met me at the airport with her husband. He stood back while we greeted each other. 'Oh my,' said my mother, like an American, standing in front of me with her hands spread open-palmed in a gesture of plenitude. 'Oh my.' Her hair was cut shorter than the last time I had seen her at the North Sydney pool, more like I remembered it from my childhood. Her face was still thin, with small bundles of wrinkles starting to gather on her cheeks and in the dimples beneath the corners of her mouth. She was still pretty and in a way I liked this face more than the previous time I had seen her. Her hair was flecked now with grey and for the first time I could see that she looked like Hil.

We shook hands. I remembered her wiry fingers with the small knotted knuckles. And then we hugged awkwardly. She gestured behind her and Ted, I remembered his name, stepped forward a little apologetically, a tall soft-skinned, peaceful-faced man, who picked up my cases and walked ahead like a chauffeur, parting the crowd quietly before us.

They lived in a suburb around forty-five minutes' drive away, and as we drove we chatted about my flight, which had been delayed, and then the weather, which was unseasonably dry, and then the eldest son Hamish's cello lessons and the possibility that he might have a girlfriend about whom he was saying nothing. This information, added my mother, had come from the younger son, Kit, and might not be reliable. I sat in the back and as Ted drove I saw my mother reach her hand across and place it on his and saw him glance quickly at her and smile.

No one else was home when we arrived, for which I was

thankful. My mother led me from the back door down a stone path through the garden, which contained a small rock pool and several slender eucalypts, and to her studio, which had been converted for now into my bedroom. Just outside the door, ants were converging on the path, and looking down I saw the drying remains of a small bug-eyed fledgling. My mother made a sad 'oh' sound and nudged the seething parcel gently into the grass with her foot. Inside there was a kettle and small fridge, and a single bed, for which she apologised, and shutters that I could open or close. She asked if I was hungry or thirsty and we went inside to where Ted was setting a late lunch on to the wooden table in the sunny kitchen. The sons arrived not long after.

Hamish, at fourteen, had his father's pale skin and sloping shoulders and freckles and looked directly into my eyes as he nodded his head. He said 'hi' with a half smile and slightly raised eyebrows, politely but humorously, as if to say, 'Well, here we are then—' and this broke the ice in a way that made everybody laugh. Kit, ten, was small and dark and fidgety with dirt or bruises on his knees and shins, and a baseball bat he would not put away even as he ate. He cast me small furtive glances but grinned when we finally made eye contact. He seemed like the sort of brother I could have had.

We talked for a while about this and that—my mother wanted to know about Sydney and how it had changed—and I drank a glass of white wine that Ted offered me, though I could barely taste it or feel its effects. We did not mention my father, or even Hil, and after a while I felt exhaustion rolling in upon me in blank waves and I rose and said I must sleep. My mother glanced at the clock—it was mid-afternoon—and asked should she wake me in a couple of hours but I said no, I would set my alarm. She was being kind, I knew, but I could not manage the thought of her entering the room while I slept.

When at last I lay in the small white bed, though, I could not sleep. The shutters were half closed and from outside came the sounds of children and cars and afternoon in the suburbs. I lay on my back and stared at the white ceiling and felt myself stretching tighter and tighter across the room and thought of the fledgling, the skin hard now and shiny and the tufts of dried feather that had pushed through the stubs of its tiny splayed wings. Eventually the light beyond the shutters began to fade and I pulled myself to sitting and opened my toiletry bag and washed my face in the bowl of cool water my mother had left on her cleared desk.

Inside the house, Hamish was practising his cello somewhere. My mother and Ted were talking quietly in the kitchen as he stirred at a saucepan on the stove and she stood beside him wiping a wooden board with a tea towel.

'Did you sleep?' she asked, moving towards me, and I said yes, a little, and Ted said there was soda in the fridge, or beer or wine if I preferred.

In the end the evening was partly redeemed. We ate outside on the wooden decking, the five of us, and talked steadily and quite easily. Hamish was writing an English essay on memory and forgetting in literature, and spoke clearly and with what seemed surprising composure for a person of fourteen. Kit, at the other end of the table looked up with a mouthful of food and said curiously, 'So, are you really our sister?' I shrugged and said I guessed so, and my mother turned to him and said teasingly and tenderly, 'There now, are you satisfied? She even looks like you.' Tilting her head and regarding me appraisingly. 'Don't you think, Ted?' And he nodded after consideration and said that yes, he thought so—not the colouring perhaps, but the eyes.

'And the lips,' said my mother quickly, as if she was going to say more, then half laughed, a quick expulsion, and said, 'Sorry Jessie'—she called me Jessie—'I'm afraid you've achieved mythological status for the boys.'

'No she hasn't,' said Hamish, embarrassed.

'You look different to your picture,' said Kit, looking towards the mantelpiece where I noticed for the first time the photograph taken by my mother at our last meeting by the harbour, my hair darker then, and pulled back from my face which I had half turned to the camera at her request, with an odd indeterminate expression.

'It's weird,' said Kit, 'having a sister who talks funny.'

'Look who's talking,' I reached across and prodded him in the ribs, making him wriggle. 'Oh no,' he said, laughing, holding one hand up as if to fend off further attack.

'Anyway,' he added after a moment, 'it's neat.'

As it started to get dark, Ted identified the unfamiliar birds still jostling and clacking in the trees, then talked a little about his work at the university. I supposed he must be older than my mother, his hair quite grey. They were very interested, both of them, in my life and my job, and I could tell they were proud, even Ted. My mother leaned forward across the table as I spoke, and rested her chin against the knuckles of her two hands as if I were telling her a story. After we had finished eating the boys retreated again, in what felt to me a remarkably orderly manner, carrying dishes with them to stack in the machine in the kitchen, and then on to homework or television or whatever it was they did. Kit came out a little later and sat in my mother's lap, his hard wiry boy calves knocking rhythmically against her legs until she remonstrated and he wriggled off and away.

Soon after, Ted rose and said he would try and propel Kit towards bed and that then he had some reading to do. He dipped his head in a courtly half-bow before leaving my mother and me alone at the table.

My mother poured more lemon squash into our glasses from a tall clear-plastic jug. 'How's Hil?' she asked after a pause. I shrugged, much as I had last time she had asked, and said that she was the same. Was she still running the youth centre, my mother wanted to know and I said, yes, three nights a week, and my mother nodded as if in confirmation then fell silent. Had she been happy about my coming over here to visit, she asked eventually. I said I didn't know, she hadn't said.

After a while she asked if Hil ever talked about her, and I said no, because I could think of no other way to say it.

My mother gave a tiny shrug, and the corners of her mouth twitched downward. 'I have lost my sister,' she said in a small voice, and for a moment she closed her eyes and rubbed with one finger at the bridge of her nose, before looking back up at me.

'What about you, Jessie?' she said. 'Are you happy?'

'I'm okay,' I said, and shrugged, like her, 'I'm fine.' My mother opened her mouth again as if to speak and I felt then, in a vivid lurch of fear and anticipation, that she was about to say something else, to tell me something else, but the screen door pushed open and Kit, pyjamaed and smelling of toothpaste, came and leaned into her shoulder as she sat. She circled his waist with her arm and pushed her face for a moment into his damp hair, and I took the opportunity to rise and pick up our empty glasses and say it was time for my bed.

A couple of times in the following days my mother made as if to resume the conversation we had not quite begun on the porch, but each time I found myself overcome by weariness, which I put down to jetlag. The second time I excused myself, wondering if I might also have picked up a bug on the plane over. My mother nodded slowly. Later, she said, if I felt well enough, she could show me around the city. I said I would like that.

In the days after that we did things that mothers and daughters do. We went sightseeing and rode on the trams. We drove down streets of candy-coloured houses and picked the ones in which we would like to live. We went to Macy's and my mother picked up a soft blue shirt from the top of its pile and said, 'May I buy you this?'

We drove by car east from San Francisco. It was a fine day with a wispy sky. My mother had borrowed for our trip a friend's red Mustang, and we drove with the top down, wind grabbing at our hair, precluding conversation. From time to time she would point at some landmark and shout a snatched commentary but for most of the trip we were quiet, facing into the wind. We drove into Yosemite and got out to inspect the giant redwoods. My mother asked a large American woman to photograph us and we stood side by side and smiled.

Later we parked the car and ate lunch near the river. We were high up on a silvery meadow where the vegetation receded in soft hummocks and tufts, and through which ran a river, a precise meandering channel such as you might draw in primary school, with grassy banks and clear perfect water. My mother told me that this was the place she loved most in America, and that sometimes when she was missing home—I was surprised to realise she meant

Australia—she would come here alone and walk. She looked very small as she ate her sandwich.

Nearby there was a kiosk where, along with hot dogs and the usual snacks, you could hire inflatable beds upon which to float downstream. I didn't particularly want to go, but my mother said, 'You must. We must,' and had already pulled out her purse to pay. Looking down into the river you could clearly see the curved shapes of smooth round river rocks far below. The water was so clean and so cold you felt you would hear a pebble crack before it hit the bottom.

'I'd get wet first,' said my mother, and walked without hesitation to the edge of the river and stepped in. She ducked for a moment and then reappeared and pulled herself straight out, hair plastered to her head, gasping and laughing. 'Oh my god.' She gestured for me to do the same, but I declined, trying instead to mount my airbed without causing ripples or wetting myself. The water that rushed into the dips made by my forearms and knees and then around my stomach was so cold I felt I'd been scalded. My mother laughed and I felt suddenly foolish and stranded and turned my face away as if to look downstream.

A little later, as we floated, my mother manoeuvred her lilo towards mine and bumped it gently and said my name. I glanced at her on her belly beside me; said quickly that it was glorious here, wasn't it glorious? And she said yes it was, and then I paddled closer to the bank for a minute, as if to look more closely at the vegetation.

Up ahead of us a family, a mother and father and three or four children, had joined up, each clasping another's inflatable until they spread like a colony of algae across the surface of the river and flowed downstream together, laughing recklessly and shrieking around the bends. My mother and I drifted to opposite sides of the small river but kept pace with each other. From time to time one of us would roll off our inflatable into the shock of the water and then pull ourself back on and lie again in the soft sun. As we drifted I pictured a small stone house on the meadow in which I would live, with flagstone floors and windows opening outwards towards the translucent sky and pale grasses and the dark rim of a mountain beyond. From across the channel, my mother waved to me with her fingers and I waved back. The breeze was soft and light as fingertips and we floated, each encased in our separate bubbles, side by side towards the sea.

I had planned to spend ten days in and around San Francisco and then take myself on to the East Coast and New York City. In the end I lasted less than a week before being overcome by home-sickness. It settled upon me after the trip to Yosemite, a dull expanding ache that robbed me of appetite and sleep. I think my mother suspected. She knocked one evening, came into my room and perched quietly on my bed with its white cotton spread while I sat at her desk, where I had been writing a postcard to Hil. She put her hands side by side, flat on her knees and looked up at me. 'I just wanted you to know that you mean the world to me,' she said, 'even though we don't know each other so well.'

She patted the bed, and when I sat beside her she looked at me and twisted her lips a little into an almost smile and said, 'I really am sorry.' I nodded and felt that she would have moved across and stroked my back then, had I wept, but I could not, so I thanked her all the same. She rang the airline and the next day drove me to the airport with Ted, who unloaded my luggage and held my shoulders briefly and said something kind in farewell before driving off to find a park while my mother came into the terminal with me. We hugged at the departure gate in a quite natural and spontaneous way, but I felt in my heart that both of us knew there was nothing more to say.

The wind has come up and rattles through the tops of the eucalypts, sometimes hitting the road in small gusts that send up pale clouds of powdery dirt in front of me. Bushfire weather. The sun is high; I have to walk on the edge of the trail, where the ground is roughest, to find shade. I check my watch. Two o'clock. I must be nearly there. Three kilometres an hour. Five and a half hours, minus half an hour for lunch. I must be close. It occurs to me that I might have miscalculated, that the fifteen kilometres might be closer to twenty.

The trail stretches ahead of me in a steep curve, dropping behind, angophoras holding their clumps of sparse foliage high above the road as if reluctant to cast shade. I have about three quarters of a litre of water. I have been pouring small amounts into my hands every half hour or so, moistening my face and neck, sprinkling it on my head before putting my hat on. Better save the rest for drinking. If I could just find a spring, a creek, a puddle, I would dunk my whole hat and let the water drip down my back as I walked. I would take off my shoes and let my pulsing feet rest in the cool, let the water soothe the inflammation, just for a few minutes.

Even here the water is not drinkable. The guide book warns that the water has been poisoned by the towns along the highway. Bad luck for the wallabies, but right now I'd take my chances. The map shows a darting line of blue running parallel to the track. A kilometre away, maybe two; you'd just head straight down through the bush.

That is how people die.

It is not, I tell myself, an emergency. I am not in danger. I am on the track. I am nearly there. But with the heat and the sapping dry and the wind all around, it is—I allow myself to know this much—like an emergency. It is what an emergency could be. (Everything suddenly tipping.) My brain tells me I am safe, about to be safe. My body is close to panic.

'You mean, you,' says Anna. 'You are close to panic.'

I keep thinking of Kit, my brother, who must now be nearing twenty, who may even have his own family, his own children, but who I see, nevertheless, as I saw him then, with his fidgety knees and his sudden sweet smile and my mother's arms wrapped around him. I think too about the older boy, Hamish, the cellist. But it is Kit I worry about.

I realise that I am very hot and that my chest is tight, and that I am hungry. The throbbing from my sole has spread up across the top of my foot and towards my calf. Just pressure, I tell myself, not an infection. Yet I understand that a visceral calculation is at work within me, despite me, weighing available resources (nutrients, water, oxygen, fitness) and current energy demands (I must keep walking) against the system's ability to metabolise energy, disperse heat, maintain blood sugar levels, keep me standing. My chest is tight. I am not well enough prepared. I need to stop. I need to sit down.

I take off my pack, a little dizzy now, nauseous, and notice that my legs are shaking as I bend down. I sit on the ground beneath a tree. I lean forwards, put my head between my knees and see dark light behind my eyes.

'You should be more careful,' says Michael.

His voice is very clear, as if he were next to me, quite gentle;

206

an observation. I understand too, at last, that it is not his voice, not Michael's voice; it is my own. I should be more careful. I should take better care.

After a minute or two I stand and bend, intending to pick up my backpack and haul it on. Instead, I take it by the shoulder straps and throw it as hard as I can along the road ahead of me. It lands with a scraping sound and I run after it and brace myself before throwing it again, harder this time, back the way I have come. When I reach it again, heart thumping and skin scratchy now and hot, I begin to kick. I kick the backpack rhythmically and methodically up one side, and down the other. I kick the frame and the bulging pockets and the tent where it sticks out the top, then I turn it over and start again, half kicking, half stamping. A couple more kicks, losing force, and then I drop to all fours in the yellow dirt and retch.

I want suddenly and powerfully for Hil to be here with me. As she always has.

When I am done, I pull myself slowly to standing. With the tip of my boot I dig out a little sandy soil from the track and kick it over the sick. Then I open the remaining part-bottle of water and take two swigs. The first I swill and spit, the second I swallow. Then I pull on my pack and keep walking.

'I wonder,' said Anna, 'if we might do an exercise.

'Would you like to do an exercise?'

I shrugged. Anna shrugged back at me.

I looked away again. Anna said nothing.

Eventually I looked back at her. She was watching me, head tilted slightly to one side, quizzical.

I smiled a little, and Anna smiled.

'Yes?' she said.

'Okay.'

'Yes then.'

Anna gestured to the mat on the floor and I lay as she told me to on my back. Start slowly, she said, just kicking the legs slowly, one by one, keep the legs straight, feeling the contact with the heels. Then add the arms, not too fast, up in the air then down by your side, right arm with left leg, left arm with right leg, thumpity thump. Thump. I stopped.

'Keep going,' said Anna. 'Just do it at your own pace.'

'I don't like it.'

'It's just unusual,' she said. 'Try making a rhythm.'

I didn't move.

'Why don't you try it again?' said Anna, looking down at me where I lay.

'Because it's stupid. Because it feels stupid.'

'Just your legs, then. Try kicking your legs again slowly, and say "stupid". Say "stupid" while you kick.'

'Stupid.' Thump. 'Stupid.' Thump. 'Stupid. There, are you happy now?' Thump.

'Don't stop. Keep going. Why do you ask?'

'Well, I'm doing what you want, aren't I?' Thump.

'I wouldn't say you were putting your heart into it, no.'

'Then stop looking at me. I can't do it while you're looking at me.' Thump. Thump. Slowly. Thump. 'It's bad enough having every-one here looking at me all the time. Now I have to put up with you staring at me too.'

'What do you have to put up with?'

'You. Looking at me. Judging me.'

'What makes you think I'm judging you? Why don't you lie down again, Jess. Keep going. Don't stop. In what way do you think I'm judging you?'

'The same way as everyone else. I'm not doing this any more.' I sat up.

'It's up to you.' Anna stepped away from the mat as I pulled myself to standing. She walked to her chair and sat down. 'I am very sure though, Jess, that I am not judging you.' Her voice was light and cool. 'Perhaps,' she shrugged slightly, 'it is you who's doing the judging.'

A sudden spurt of heat filled my throat and I wheeled abruptly towards her, unchecked. 'Well of course I bloody am,' I had raised my voice. 'Sigmund fucking Freud! Tell me something I don't know already!' Almost shouting. 'I'm sorry,' I said quickly, 'I didn't mean—'

Anna sat very still. An expression crossed her face that might have been hurt, or just surprise.

'I do exist, you know, Jess,' she said at last in what seemed to me a small tight voice. 'I'm not a figment of your imagination. I am actually here.'

There was a knock on the door. Anna rose and walked without looking at me to open it. From behind me I heard Viv's voice, then Anna's.

'Excuse me Jess,' said Anna. I swivelled in my chair and she turned to me with the door still ajar. 'I must move my car, I'm sorry.'

She seemed to be away a long time. The room was thick around me. When at last she returned she apologised again and sat down, regarded me, head tilted slightly. 'Well then,' she said.

'I thought you'd gone,' I said. And then I was crying.

I felt as if I was breaking in two. I felt that my sobs, which rose quickly into a series of gasping wails, would blast me apart, a burning river bisecting my lungs. I was curled now in my chair opposite her, face streaming with tears and snot. I could barely breathe. I must slow. I can't breathe. I looked at Anna. She was looking at me.

She said, 'Jess—'

I cut her off. I could feel the panic rising with my voice, high and windy. I said, 'Will you hold me? Can you hold me? I need to be held.'

'Jess,' she said. 'I want you to do something.' She was talking very calmly and she had not moved. 'I want you to keep looking at me. Look back here, Jess. That's right. I want you to keep looking at me, and I want you to breathe. Just for a minute. Feel your arms and legs. Jess? Come back to my eyes, Jess.'

She does not want me.

I felt myself start streaming out through the back of my head, as if a cord that had been there all the time had at last inevitably been pulled, and I was falling backwards, toppling over and over from the force of the rebuff.

'Jess, look at me.' Anna's voice in the distance was steady. 'I want you to look at me.'

Instead I grappled my way out of the chair, making clumsy flailing movements with my arms and backing away from her.

It was only then that she stood. For a moment she looked old; not beautiful; helpless. She held her hands in front of her, palms open and upturned as if to show that she meant no harm.

'Jess,' she said again, and took a small step closer, stretched her arms slightly towards me. I only saw this later, this movement, when I thought back over what had happened. At the time all I felt was the great surging fright, a kind of vertigo, and some other knowledge that I could not yet name.

'Stay away from me,' I said, 'don't come near. I have to, you have to, I—' The room is too small. There is no room. 'I have to run.'

She didn't say anything then. She stood as she was, quite close, arms now loosely by her sides and she looked at me, neither harsh nor soft. She looked at me, and I at her, and after a long moment, still without taking her eyes from mine, she lowered her head, the shadow of a nod, and I wheeled away from her then, didn't look back, yanked open the door and ran from her down the corridor, through the glass-panelled doors, into the car park and down the gravel driveway. I ran because I had nowhere to go and because once I had started I had to keep running.

I was half way up my hill before I stopped. I sank on to a grassy hummock; the soil around me was pale and dry; my heart was thudding. After a while, when it settled, I got up and began to make my way back down the path, slow at first, then gathering pace until I arrived at the front gates at a lope. I stopped on the driveway to regain my breath, and walked the last fifty metres to the back door more slowly, then along the corridor to her room.

She was sitting in her chair, waiting. She looked up when she heard me, and I crossed the room and sat on the floor beside her, arms around my knees, pressing the side of my body into her leg, her flank. She rested the back of her hand, her loosely curled fingers, briefly against my cheek. After a moment I let my head drop on to her lap, and she stroked my hair slowly from my face and kept stroking, and neither of us spoke.

*

The phone starts ringing again. I reach into the pack and check the number before answering.

'Hello Laura.'

'Jessica, I'm sorry, I've been foolish—'

'No you—'

'Yes, I have. I want to apologise. I've been pushy and intrusive and unforgivably insensitive.'

'I don't—'

'No, hear me out, Jessica, really. Viv at the nursing home told me you were taking some time alone to think, and I just blundered in anyway because it suited me. My husband ripped into me this afternoon and he was right. He was! And thank god I've got him. I'm afraid I haven't coped well with what's been happening with Hugh—and I know, how can I be expected to, it's been a stressful time, etcetera etcetera, I know all that—but really, sometimes I just go on and on and make things worse, and now—'

'Laura, can you just shut up a minute?'

She halts abruptly, then starts up again. 'See, I'm doing it again. I—'

'Laura, I'm not offended. I don't feel intruded upon. You made a kind offer. Yes, you're talking very fast. No, I don't think you're unforgivably insensitive. No, I don't think I'm doing any better with my own life. In fact, compared with you I'm a disaster. You're just trying to look after your children, you're doing your best.'

She is quiet for a while and when she speaks again her voice is slower.

'The truth is Jessica that neither of my children want me anywhere near them.'

'Well I'm sure—'

'My daughter's heading back to London this week, and Hugh wouldn't even come with us. He's had them move him to a rehab place in Sydney, and as soon as he's fit he says he's going back to Melbourne. He told me to come home. Dad's going down to see him tomorrow, but Hugh doesn't even want me to come. That's how good a mother I've been.'

'Well,' I say at last. 'You seem like a nice mother to me.'

'Yes.' Dismissive. 'Jessica,' she says after a pause. 'Your daughter—I'm sorry, they said you had a little girl—you can tell me to stop.'

'Lily.'

'You know, I wasn't being rash about staying here, about the flat. I'm a quick judge of character and I'm usually right. It really is beautiful here, we're on the river. You could bring her. You could stay for as long as you liked. I wouldn't, you know, be a bother.'

I have a sudden vision of a room among trees on a river bend, a wall of glass and stippled light.

'Laura, I—thank-you. Right now though I really need to—'

'You don't have to answer. I just want you to know it's there.'

'I have to talk to my husband.'

'Yes of course. And your daughter, you must get back to your daughter.' She pauses. 'Jessica,' she says, 'you will get back to your daughter, won't you?'

In the silence after her question I watch a small brown bird on the side of the road beat its wings against the dry ground, producing a halo of yellow dust in which it continues to dip and flap as if hoping for water. Suddenly I want to tell her what a failure I've been. How I have let down my daughter, my precious child, whose very existence portends loss. How I have married a man I can neither like nor leave. I want to tell her everything. To wrap myself in her pure imperfect love and seek absolution.

'Perhaps we could visit,' I say at last. 'Perhaps—'

But the phone has died. I push it back deep into the bag and continue.

Dear mummy, writes Lily, *Nancy starfish should make friends with the Nuthing.*

A car is coming. Through the thudding of blood in my ears the new sound accumulates, takes shape. I look up and see at first nothing, trees. Then dust rising around the bend up the hill ahead of me, a glint of silver. It is travelling quite slowly, taking up the road, dirty white behind the roo bar. I pull myself to standing. It is going the wrong way, down the mountain, but I want it to see me; I want to be seen. I want to ask how far it is to the end. I step out a little into the road, and raise my hand. The car slows, then stops. There is just the driver, a man. He winds down the window and puts his head out. A straight blokey face, a little weight around the chin and neck. Brown hair, cut short. Mid-forties. Familiar somehow. He says, 'Hello again.' I suppose I must stare.

'We passed you on the way out,' he says. 'I had my wife and the kids in the car. You spoke to my wife.'

The family. He is the father. I am confused. Why is he here?

'Can you tell me how far it is,' I ask, 'to the end?'

'Couple of kilometres. All uphill. Hop in, I'll give you a lift. Too hot to be walking.'

'Where are your children?' Uneasy.

'All up at the picnic ground,' he says, gesturing back the way he's come. 'Jane, my wife, told me to come and make sure you were all right. Too hot out here.'

He is not that much older than me, but he seems a generation away. A father. He has come to get me. I pick up my pack and he hops out, comes around, opens the back door and puts it on the seat. 'Must've been getting heavy. Bill,' he says, and puts out a hand, a solid paddle, which I shake.

'I'm Jessica.'

Bill opens the passenger door for me to climb in. He closes his door, and his window slides up at the touch of a button. The air is cool and conditioned. There is a wider patch of road about one hundred metres down the incline, where he reverses and turns the car, and then we are all uphill, pulling and crunching over small rocks and twigs, potholes, ridges. 'You're like a knight,' I say. 'From a book.'

'That's what they say.'

At the picnic area the mother, Jane, is crouching at the base of a stone wall with the two children. The stones are flat, laid out in slices, and in the cracks are tiny lizards, skinks, which dart in and out of the shadows, gleaming like copper. A toddler and an older girl squat back on their heels like their mother. Jack and Amy. They have twigs in their hands, and now and then they poke carefully into the cracks, hoping to provoke some creature into breaking its cover. Or perhaps just to impale them. 'Gentle. Be gentle,' their mother keeps saying, although she doesn't tell them to stop. Perhaps she is weighing the risk of injury to the skinks against the benefit of diversion for her children. But crouched beneath her straw hat she seems contented, engaged, and I think, this is what children do, this is what millennia of children have done.

She smiles as I approach, introduces herself, although I already know her name. I say, 'Thank you for saving me.'

She ducks her head. 'Too hot, too windy. Bill and I used to bushwalk before—' she gestures to the children. She doesn't ask about my imaginary friend. 'I didn't like thinking of you alone, and we were coming back this way anyway.' A shrug. 'There's a stream over there.'

I have already taken off my shoes and socks and now I hobble across the dusty car park in the direction she has pointed.

'Hang on,' she calls, 'we'll come.'

The water is shallow, just over the tops of my feet, and so cold that when I touch it with the soles of my feet it feels electric. 'God that's good,' I say.

'You bet,' says Jane, sitting on a rock a little further along the bank, pulling off her own shoes.

'Od ood,' says Jack, regarding me gravely. Amy sits down next to me, proprietorial, and bursts into a peal of exaggerated laughter. 'He can't even talk properly yet,' she tells me. 'But you can say my name, can't you? What's my name Jack? What's my name?' Jack looks at her for a while, expressionless, then says 'mee-mee', before heading suddenly at a run for the water.

'No you don't,' says Jane, catching him by one arm at the stream's edge. 'Let me take those shoes off.'

'He said my name Mum, did you hear him say my name?'

Soon we are all sitting there, dangling, as if we have known each other longer than fifteen minutes. Long enough not to need to talk much. 'Can you do plaits, Jess?' says Amy. 'Can you plait my hair?' And without waiting for an answer she wriggles over to sit cross-legged in front of me. I look down at the top of her head, the ragged parting, the white skin beneath, and I have the strange brief sense that a hand has been pushed through my solar plexus up into the cavity of my chest and is clenching now where the heart must be, my heart, so that an ache spreads outwards towards my throat and my stomach and I realise with surprise, Oh, that is grief. This is grief.

Jane says, 'Where do you live, Jess?'

'Sydney. Bondi. But I've been away.'

(Where do I live? Where will I live? What am I doing?)

Then I say to myself, one step at a time, one foot in front of the other, and I take a segment of the girl's fine hair and divide it into three.

Jane is beautiful. Narrow-bodied with reddish brown hair in a bob that swings along the line of her jawbone, and tiny white creases leading away from her eyes. I think, that is how I would like to be in ten years. She has a quick, poised concentration, and her arms and legs beneath her sarong are brown and finely muscled. She is crouched now on the edge of the water with the little boy, and while she talks to me she lifts handfuls of tiny river rocks, opens her palm in front of his face like a shell or a flower and lets him knock them, ping ping, back into the water. It has been hard for her, it occurs to me, to learn to be still, to wait and be patient. But she has learned. Her calves support the backs of her thighs as she squats with the boy in the late sun, restful and alert.

I look around for Bill. He is not at the car or the picnic table. 'He's gone for a walk,' says Jane. 'There's a walk near here he likes to do. We used to do it together, now we take turns.'

'I want to go with Daddy,' says Amy suddenly, sitting upright, pulling her head away from me, plaits forgotten. She looks at her mother with an expression passionate and accusing. 'You said I could go with him.'

'But you came with us instead, to the water.'

'I didn't know he was going. I wanted to go with him.' She is wailing now, half risen.

'You can go with him next time, Amy.'

'No. Now. I'm going to catch him.' She leaps back on to the bank and starts at a run towards the car park.

'Amy.' Jane's voice is sharp. 'Look where you're going. You can't follow Daddy.'

She too has risen and swings Jack towards me by his upper arms, following Amy, like a markswoman, with her eyes. 'Just a moment.'

She too sets off running. 'Amy. Stop there!'

She catches up with her on the other side of the car park at the top of the steps leading down to the walking track. I see them standing beneath a tree, a vivid tableau, the girl stamping her foot, trying to break free of the mother who has her by the wrist. When they get back, Amy doesn't speak, she takes herself to a spot further along the creek and sits with her back to us looking in the direction her father has gone. Jane looks at me and rolls her eyes. 'I'm the witch.'

It is getting towards the end of the day. Bill comes back from his walk. Away from the car he looks younger, freer. His hair is wet as though he has swum or dipped it into a pool. Amy jumps up and runs towards him, calling, and wraps her arms extravagantly around his waist. I see now that he is attractive, pretending to stagger backwards under the impact of her embrace, lifting her, sack-like, to his shoulders ('Daddy, Daddy,' she chants), grinning at Jane, who raises her eyebrows and smiles back at him quizzically. I wonder if they still have sex. The toddler, Jack, drops backwards on his bottom and starts to cry.

'Tired,' says Jane, bending to lift him.

They are staying a few kilometres away with Jane's sister. Can they drop me somewhere? Where am I staying? I don't know. There is a motel nearby, I know, and I murmur something about a phone, if they could just drop me at a phone, I can walk from there, or get a taxi. But I am thinking, it must be near to here. I am nearly at the place where we came that day. My foot feels possible again, shrunk to a manageable discomfort.

'You just calling the motel?' says Bill, reaching into his pocket. 'Here, use the mobile.'

But I say, no, it may be a longer call. And after a moment, because it is true, I say, 'I'm going to call my husband.'

Jane looks at me with her clear grey eyes and nods. Bill, perhaps at some instruction, jogs on ahead to the car, Amy still slung squealing around his neck. Jane walks beside me, holding Jack, whose head is drooping now on to her shoulder.

'When we lost our first son,' she says, 'I thought I would never have another child. I thought I could not bear it, to love like that again. But I did, you see.'

I thank her. I don't tell her that is not what happened to me.

*

At the last instant, just before we come off the dirt road, I lean forwards and ask Bill to stop the car. 'I can walk from here.'

'You sure? We're nearly there.' He slows and pulls to the side of the road, swivels towards me.

'Yep. Thanks.'

I nod at Jane, who has turned too and is looking at me, eyes slightly narrowed in inquiry. 'I need the exercise,' I say, and we all laugh, tension broken, and I open the door and climb out.

Jack has started to cry again. Jane reaches behind, fishes with an arm around his seat. Bill comes across and opens the boot, pulls out my pack and leans it against the side of the car for me. He says, 'Good luck,' and puts out his hand, which I shake again. He doesn't quite meet my eye, and I think: he is afraid of women who need saving; that is why he married Jane. I say, 'No, I'm fine,' and Jane opens the door, climbs out. I think at first she too is going to shake my hand. She stands in front of me for a moment, then steps quickly into a hug. I feel her shoulder blade and stroke her T-shirt, once, twice, over the bone, before she steps back. Jack is hiccoughing now with distress or frustration, and she turns, ducks smoothly back into her seat to pass a litre bottle of water out to me through the window. In the back, Amy reaches across the crying child and winds down the window a couple of inches.

'Bye-bye Jess, goodbye.' As if suddenly, again, we are family. I blow her a kiss as the car draws away. Stand for a moment on the side of the road, feeling—what?—uncertain, un-something.

I am on the highway before I know it. A truck sputters past, a blurred line of sound and scattered twigs. I step back. I can't have been walking more than ten minutes. Fifteen, tops. Ridiculous. For a moment I think about heading back the way I have come, charging back towards the line of gums, but there's no point really. I am here, on the road, not in the wilds. I am on the main highway and metres away I now notice, on the other side of the road, is a line of shops, a bakery, the corner pub. I am in a town.

When the road is clear I cross, the bitumen flat and unyielding, a small line of pain in my hip. If that cafe is open, I will have a coffee. Sit down, read a magazine, think about what to do next. The sign in the glass door says welcome, a cuckoo clock in one window. But as I am about to enter, the door opens from inside and a couple, man and wife, come out. The man reaches back to turn the sign to closed and locks the door from outside. The woman catches my eye, shrugs. She might be about to say something but she sees someone beyond me, smiles across me, waves. They set off in a group, the cafe couple, the waved-to woman, a large boy of sixteen or so, shoulders huge in his padded jacket, walking together up the highway, leaving me feeling small, unkind. The woman from the cafe has a knitted woollen beret, plum-coloured, that looks like a tea cosy. I am flooded suddenly with distaste. The thought of living like this, of choosing that hat, of displaying that clock. The boy with his great round bulk bringing up the rear of the group. The gap between us stretching and chilling and the whoosh of cars passing me from behind, heading home from the city.

I turn and start to walk away from them, back down the mountain. There must be somewhere else. About fifty metres on there is a road to the left, which leads, I realise, to the shopping centre and the station. I pass a real estate agent, a bookshop; glance in the window of a bric-a-brac store with small knitted animals in the window. I am almost past it before I realise there are tables and chairs in there, and people sitting. Inside, it is gloomy, the lights not yet on, and I have to pick my way over to the counter to make out the menu on the blackboard above it. I order a latte from a man with a long sad moustache, and the remaining slice of cake. Carrot or banana with thick damp icing which I will remove.

There is only one group in the café, and turning back into the room I see now that they are Aboriginal, or most of them are Aboriginal. They have pulled two or three small tables together and are sitting in a cluster laughing quite loudly at something one of them has said. There are a couple of white people to one end—two boys, dreadlocked and nose-ringed, one with his hair tied above his head in a spray—and another, a woman, in the middle of the group, sitting with her back to me. I know her. I know her broad back, and her long dark hair (loose now) and her voice, which is throaty with laughter. I am about to look away when she turns and stares straight at me. Steff. Her eyes rest on me for a moment, almost absently, then she turns with a fluid motion back towards the group.

The sun is dropping outside as I leave, and a small cold wind is leaking into the street from the direction of the highway. Overhead the cloud is clumping together. Looking beyond me along the rail track, I see that it has settled already into a low flat ceiling that darkens and gathers intensity with distance. At the far edge it is purple. It has happened without my noticing, and only now, with the warmth and light beginning to drain, do I let myself know that I must make a decision. I bend and pull my map from the side of my pack. I think I know where the path is, and once there I think I know how to get to the place. I don't know how I know, or where I get the unfamiliar sense of certainty. I have been here only once before. But I know where I am going. I will need a lift to the start of the walking tracks, which these days begin, the map shows me, from a large car park. And then perhaps half an hour to walk to the place. It needn't take long. I could be there and back before dark. If I wanted. I could be there tonight.

Further along the street is the station where there will be a phone and probably a taxi rank. The cab could drop me at the car park at the start of the walk. I know that the weather is against me, and the light. I know I could stay in the pub, or a hostel, or a hotel. I have MasterCard. I have Visa. In my pack I have a litre of water, a packet of Continental chicken soup, half a loaf of bread and a banana; I could stay the night in the bush. If I find it, if I found the place, I could stay the night. I wouldn't even need the tent. It wouldn't matter. Even if I didn't find it, it would be all right.

There is a payphone next to the empty taxi rank outside the station and I shrug off the pack, reach into the side pocket and pull out my change: one twenty, one fifty cent piece. Hil doesn't answer so I leave a message on her mobile. I tell her where I am and not to worry. When I finish, a cab is sitting in the rank. A train draws in below in the cutting, and I hurry now to reach the taxi before someone else takes it. The driver has the door open, his feet on the road, smoking a cigarette. He stubs it out when he sees me coming, grinds it, swings his body heavily back inside.

'You'll be after the resort?' he says, unsmiling, looking me up and down through the window. My dirty shorts. My backpack. He has a thick neck with reddish brown folds, and a head of grey stubble. It takes me a moment to realise he is joking, that this is his idea of a joke. I say, no I want to go to where the walks start. He shrugs; says hop in then.

'Which walk?' After we have been driving a few minutes.

'The one from the car park, the path along the top.'

'Which car park?'

I realise that he isn't going to help me, that I have to do this alone.

'Just take me to the closest one.' If it is not this car park, he can take me to the next. Or the next. I say nothing. He shrugs. Turns the radio on. Tiny splatters of rain start to fall on the windscreen. And a minute later we are there, entering down a one-way road that leads to a bitumen parking area, empty now of cars. The fare is $4.50 and I give him five, knowing that he will not give me change without me asking, and knowing that I will not ask. Except that when it comes to it I find myself sitting in the back waiting, with my hand held out, until he passes fifty cents back to me without turning. I am afflicted almost immediately by doubt. This petty power play. And him not rich, probably poor. I try to give it back, as if I had never intended him to return it, muttering, 'No, no, it's okay.'

But he ignores me, setting his back against me, and after a moment I clamber out and pull the pack behind me. Threads of

226

thin bad feeling. He starts to draw away the instant the door is closed and I find myself suddenly thumping on the car's boot, once, twice, with the palm of my hand. He stops. I walk around the back of the car to his window. He looks at me, impassive. I hold his gaze. I hear my voice, very clear and earnest, as if this is information that he too has been seeking. 'I came here with my mother when I was a child.'

I say it twice. Nodding my head and looking at him. And after a moment he too dips his head, once, twice. And draws away, this time more slowly.

When he has gone, when I can no longer see his car, I squat and pull my rain jacket from my pack. It is spitting only lightly and the weather may yet move off, I tell myself, although I can feel the chill rising from the valley below. It is about half a kilometre back to where the walks start, and there is a large sign with a map showing the various tracks laid out in dots and dashes, blue and red and brown. The map shows a set of stairs you can follow, doubling back and forth upon itself, clinging to the cliff face, right to the bottom of the escarpment. From there, other walks follow the base of the cliff, or strike west into the valley a kilometre below. Down there is wilderness.

There is another track, about half way down, that looks to have been gouged into the cliff face, impossibly high and narrow, a ledge made for birds, not people. There are shorter walks too, up the top. One to a waterfall, another that travels for a while beneath the overhanging sandstone lip of the escarpment. That sounds right. But the more I look at the map, the less certain I become. The less sure even that I am at the right place. I feel in my body the tight coil of anxiety. Who will tell me? Who will show me the way?

I stop looking. I decide to follow my nose.

Up here the steps are wide and broad, packed with earth, held with railway sleepers. I take them one at a time, giant steps. None of it is familiar. Except the earth, slightly moist now and exuding a tired, end of day, dog smell. A small path opens off to the right. I stop, undecided. It is the right direction, I am sure, but narrow and overgrown. I take a few paces along, then a few more and end up following it a couple of hundred metres before the way is blocked by an upturned tree trunk. But even before the tree I know it is not right. I push my way back between clumps of damp grass and continue down the steps until the next pathway. I turn on to it before I even give myself time to think, and enter suddenly into a cool vast knowledge. I do not think it. It is just there.

For so much of my life I have not known where I was going—not let myself know where I was going—and here now, in this moment, my certainty is unavoidable. The doubt is a decoy. The map, the checking for signs; all of it is decorative, a distraction. The taxi driver, too, the drama over the change. Even the walk up the mountain. I know where I am going. I have known since I left the nursing home. Since before then; since waking up from the coma. Even, the thought striking itself like a black flame, the coma. Now shrunk. Irrelevant. I no longer look at the vegetation around me or check for reference points. I do not care any more where I am going. I just know that I am going there. I am powered by a great silence in the back of my skull. I know where I am going. And suddenly, as quickly as it came, the feeling is gone. Not a feeling: a knowledge, a place, an opening in my mind through which I have seen, for a moment, clearly.

I am standing in front of a deep rocky overhang. A cave. It is where I came before she went away. It is raining. Now that I am here, there seems nothing extraordinary about the place, or even the fact of my arrival. It is close to dark, and I could not honestly say that it looks the same as it did back then, that I would recognise it in a photo, or even identify the ways in which it has changed; though the trees must surely be higher. The escarpment is not apparent in the rain and the mist; I just know that it is there. And this knowledge may not even be knowing, it may simply be a decision. It doesn't matter. I am here.

VI

I step in under cover, shrug off first my backpack, then my rain jacket. Then I sit under the rock over-hang, watching the rain as it slides off down the valley away from me. I think, 'I am sheltering from the rain.' It is big in here. Not quite a cave but a deep wedge, high enough, even this far in, for a person to stand. For people to stand.

I think again of Steff, standing with her back against my door the day before I left. Her low tight voice.

'You ought to be ashamed of yourself.'

I didn't say anything, my stomach tightened. I sat on my bed and waited. I knew that whatever she was going to say would not surprise me. The room shrank around her and she shook it slowly with her head.

'It's fucking disgusting. That's what I think. There's people spend their whole lives trying to find their kids, you know that? Kids who spend their whole lives trying to find mothers, fathers, aunties, anyone. You wouldn't have a clue, would you?'

She took a step away from the door, into the room. Practically hissed the next bit. 'Think you'll go walkabout do you? Try and find yourself?'

I raised my hand to my mouth. There was a sound caught in the back of my throat. Steff thrust one hand forward, like a policeman, as if to stop me speaking. I cleared my throat, but I had nothing to say.

'Well let me tell you sister,' she said at last, 'you're just buying time, and you're buying it with pain. Other people's pain.' She paused and said at last the thing she had wanted to say. 'Your little girl's pain.'

The cave is cool and quiet, protected from the weather. Outside the sky is a dense grey sheet. Steff, with her broad face and dark eyes. Her white skin. White, but not like me. That is what she was telling me: she would never be like me. She crossed the room, passing my bed on the way to the window, knocking a pile of folded clothes to the floor. She didn't stop. Reached the window and opened it wide, as if to let in clean air.

'Got what you wanted, didn't you? They all feel sorry for you.' She spoke conversationally, turning back into the room. She raised her voice now that she had said what she needed to. 'Bet you've been wanting people to feel sorry for you your whole life, haven't you?' She looked straight at me, held my gaze. 'Yeah, you have.' She shook her head. 'Unbelievable.'

*

There is a darkened patch on the rock ceiling. At first I think it might be damp, a seeping crack, but looking down I see a smudge of charcoal and below it burnt sticks. If I started now I could be at the station in an hour or so. Or I could head back to the main road and find myself a hotel for the night. In the gloom, I squat and pick up a blackened twig, clear a space on the rock floor, draw a heart, a feathered arrow. Love heart. Stupid. I rub it out. On the wall behind me I find scratched initials, a charcoal cock and balls. Primitive rock art. The rock floor is coated with a dry, sandy residue that might one day become soil. There is a broad flat area next to the fireplace. I open my pack and unroll my sleeping mat. Pull out my stove, lamp, matches. No one will pass now; not before morning.

After I have spread the sleeping bag on the thin blue mat, I find a flat rock where I place the stove and half fill the saucepan with water from the rock face outside. I fish out a couple of small pieces of vegetation, leaving a brown sediment in the bottom. I get the packet of soup from the backpack and reach for the matches to light the stove, but in the end I don't.

It is that indeterminate time between dusk and nightfall, when nothing can be done. When it feels that nothing can be done but wait. I pull another jumper from the pack and carry my sleeping bag to the mouth of the cave. Cave. I say it again. Try to make it solid. I am sitting at the mouth of the cave. I am looking out. I pull my knees up to my chest and the rain falls steadily, settling in for the night.

The ants too are seeking shelter. A wavering column. They clamber singly and in pairs up the wet moss outside the cave, in under the rocky overhang, antennae still flattened against their heads. Outside, the water washes down the rock face, parting around the mossy outcrops as if they were eyebrows. They are larger than the ants at the nursing home, these ones. Reddish brown rather than black, but they work with the same purpose, moving impossibly fast for their size, most of them clasping above them one, sometimes two, spherical milky eggs. They thin out as night approaches and disappear, as ants do, almost magically. The file fading, then gone. This is the first rain I remember, heavy rain, since I woke up.

Sitting here now on the edge of a cave in the rain, I am reminded suddenly of that first exercise with Anna, jiggling up and down in the room with the three old women. The feeling of my legs afterwards, heavy and boneless. That is how it feels now. The memory locates itself in my body, so that even as I look down and see my legs clearly outlined before me, I experience them only as a distant formless buzzing. And I see again my mother's dark hair floating in a ring on the water.

I sit for a long time in the gathering dark. At first the feeling is so strong, so convincing, that I believe I cannot walk. I think I will have to wait until someone passes by tomorrow and ask them to call me an ambulance. Then I think that I will be dead before then, that I will not be able to endure being like this: the crawling, swarming pain in my legs and pelvis, the feeling of darkness and badness that wraps itself all around me, my throat and face. The certainty that this is not survivable. I think that I am bad. A bad seed. I think that it is my fault. Eventually I start to notice the thoughts and that I am thinking them, and that behind the thoughts is the feeling, just sitting there, as familiar as day, not doing anything in particular.

In the darkness a new memory begins to cohere around me, less memory than sensation, pressed and fingered out of the blackness that now surrounds me (the hard vault of the cave), easing its way through the body's grammar, expanding into the flaring parentheses of the ribs, nudging through the body's contraction (the heart), reprising, reclaiming its form (now opening, relinquishing the child.

I am five. I am in a cave. I am waiting for my mother.

When I awoke it was black. A darkness so thick it displaced all else. No thought or name or word. No throat or tongue. Just darkness and pressure and after a while a rhythmic gathering and collapsing, forming and unforming. Sound/ Sobbing/ Self.

I did not try to move, that night all those years ago. Nor did I try to stop the sound, a slow low murmuring. I could not tell if my eyes were open or closed so I pressed them together to find their edges. I could feel the rock hard against my bottom and back, which were wedged still into the rear of the cave. In the darkness I could no longer tell where I ended or the darkness began. I was the cave and the darkness was inside me. Even my breath, a wet panting, seemed as if it came from somewhere or something much bigger. I whimpered for my mother. I said her name, the name I called her, and in the saying (the syllables moulded and pressed forth from my mouth) I felt myself come into focus. This was me; everything else was the desire for my mother. There was me and there was my wanting. I was oddly comforted by the wanting, and the knowing that it was mine, and the recognition that this meant that I existed, and that she did too. I stroked myself softly with the small blunt syllables and after a while I had the powerful sense that I was no longer alone, that my mother whom I had summoned up with my crooning was now with me. I felt

236

that as I lay curled in the cave she lay curled around me, filling my chest with her breathing, enveloping me in a rich golden light. And once again I slept.

My daughter was born on a Thursday, at daybreak. 'Seems a bit unfair doesn't it,' said the nurse who brought me breakfast afterwards, 'to go so long and not even remember the birth.' But I didn't mind, not at the time; it had been a relief, my birth plan abandoned (the CDs, the oil burner still in a bag in the corner). I'd wanted drugs. I'd wanted the pain to end. Even so, when I emerged from the fog, it was hard to understand that the ancient shrouded creature in the container beside me was mine, and once or twice I found myself wondering if she was—if there might have been some error, if my child might have disappeared with someone else. I didn't tell Michael, though, nor that I had felt easier before the birth (my child held tightly within the rim of my belly), nor that some days when I looked at her all I could feel was an aching whose borders could not be patrolled.

The nurse who was trying to teach the baby to suck said that a lot of women felt this way and that I could expect to be a bit blue for a few days. When she pushed the baby's face on to my dark, enormous nipple, I worried that the child would choke. It seemed to be trying to pull its head away.

'C'mon you,' said the nurse sternly and I was not sure if she was talking to the child or to me, and either way there were great fat tears leaking down my face, plopping on to the baby's head. It didn't work anyway. There was milk but not enough and the baby was fretful.

It went on for a week or two, even when we were back in the

flat, the baby crying, me rigid, the visiting nurse insisting, the baby losing weight, Michael ringing a colleague, the nurse (eventually) backing down. It did not worry me as much as it should have. I felt safer with her in my lap, being able to see how well she was feeding, how much she had drunk from the bottle, which would not smother her, and which could be filled and cleaned at call, and which could be passed to Michael. I liked that she did not depend only on me, that she had Michael also, the two of us. One egg. Two baskets.

It was not, I tried to explain to the nurse on her last visit, that I did not want to hold my child. The nurse was worried there was a problem, and perhaps there was but it was not the one she thought.

I loved, with a feeling so powerful I am not sure, even now, if it was right (or even love—so blank and urgent) to watch my child as she slept. I leaned over the crib and inhaled her. I put my face as close as I dared to her sweet biscuity crown and breathed and breathed and breathed in the dark. She was a good sleeper; I was not. Three or four times a night I woke and stood like this beside her. I checked first to see that she was alive, that she was breathing, and then I just stayed there.

Sometimes she woke and mewled or cried and I felt guilty and soothed her and moved away. I did not want to oppress her. Once, though, she grabbed my hair with her hand, as if she knew what she was doing, and I stayed there hunched over her for what seemed like an hour until my back was screaming, though I barely noticed. I just kept breathing her in until at last it seemed that I could feel her inside me, curled in my chest, a thick treacly light.

'That's it,' Anna whispers to me now. 'That is the feeling. That is love.'

*

I think now of the day I lay down. The day that the woman Andrea visited and told me about my husband. And about what had already happened before she came: the postman on his bike and the letter from America. The letter was from Ted, forwarded unopened by Stuart. He wrote in a black pen in his old man's writing, and told me that my mother had died. (How many times, I wondered, could one woman die?) Ted wrote that she had got up as usual the Thursday before, and had eaten her breakfast and read the paper and reminded him that the boys would be over for dinner. Then she had walked up the driveway towards the car and collapsed. It was a blood clot, he said, in the brain. Just like that. He had sat with her for some hours, he wrote, on the driveway and in the ambulance and then the hospital, but she had not regained consciousness. He just hoped she knew he had been there with her. That she had known she was not alone.

It was a dignified letter, and calm and generous. My mother had always loved me, he wrote, as much as she loved the boys, and she had always believed that one day she and I would find each other again. 'You were always very much a part of our family,' he wrote, 'and always will be.' He would have rung, he said, but he didn't have my number. There were other details too, the death notice and funeral arrangements and even news of a small legacy, which they had always agreed would be mine even though, as he wrote, 'we never expected your mother to go first'.

I read the letter and put it away. I put it in the box at the top of the linen closet in which I kept all my mother's letters, from the first, to this, the last. I wrapped the box again, as I always did, in a shawl I remembered her wearing when I was a child and which I slept with for many years after she left. It is a soft lichen green, like

239

her eyes. After I had wrapped it I pushed it again to the back of the highest shelf, where no one would find it. Not even me. And after a while my head began to ache.

There is no use crying inside the cave, I know that now, so I stand outside in the rain where everything is wet and my tears are part of something bigger and I can let them come. I cry for Ted and for my little brothers, who have lost their mother, and I cry for my mother who lost hers, and for Hil and for my daughter and for myself.

Eventually I notice that my legs feel different, more normal, and that when I turn on the torch briefly and look down at them they seem sturdy and uncomplicated. I wonder what Anna would make of all this. Whether I will tell her. I think I will. The rain is slowing. It occurs to me that if I decide to go back to Michael I will need to talk a lot more and I will have to have sex. I think of my dependable husband with his shy hidden smile and his oyster eyes and the expression I could never name. And of that terrible tender revulsion that allows us to send our fingers and tongues into another's body even when that body will only leave, or die. To share the sourness of daybreak saliva (the magpies' morning cries pooling beyond the window as we kiss). To suck each other's glistening eyes and swallow. Perhaps that too is love.

As I watch, the wind starts to move the storm clouds around, starts to break them down so that I see at first the pale strong glow of the moon shining through the thinnest areas, and eventually a clear space that grows slowly larger, through which, after a while, I can see the bright white disc high up, above the wind.

'Is there anything you want from me?' asked Anna. 'Is there

anything you would like me to do?'

From here, looking up, the ring of clear sky looks like a pool of dark water in the clouds and the moon, high, high up, looks like its own reflection, gleaming back at me.

What I think now is that I would like to touch her face. What I want to do is to touch her face, her eyes. I want to touch around her eyes with the soft pads of my fingers. I would like to press the pads of my fingers softly beneath her eyes, follow the ring of bone around, rest my fingertips quietly against the creases.

After a while I notice, just inside the cave, a pile of twigs, kindling, and beyond, several larger pieces of wood. The rain has stopped. I pull the broken branches on to the damp flat rock outside and light myself a fire. I cook the soup first and when the fire is hot enough and the bigger sticks have become embers, I push the banana in and let it cook until the skin is black; the flesh inside sweet and pulpy. Like my mother used to do. Bananas and ice-cream. Mother. I let myself think properly at last about my own little girl, about Lily—whether it is true, as I have tried to tell myself, that she will be better without me. And I answer myself with the answer I have known all along.

In the darkness, my daughter arrives quietly, unsurprisingly, fully formed. She has toes and feet and five-year-old fingers with tiny shredded nails. She has elbow joints, hip sockets, knuckles—all connected by gristle and muscle and hot dry skin. She has green eyes and that lustrous ludicrous hair. She smells of metal or rasp-berries, I never can decide. She throws her thin arms around my neck and pulls me against her so hard it hurts. She is all angles. She is very serious. She says, My mummy. I am hers.

*

I used to say to Anna, when she asked about her, 'My mother did this' or 'My mother did that'; always, 'my mother': my mother hated sewing, my mother had one of those faces. People used to stare. Even in the street, even as a small child, I remember the feeling. Of her being looked at.

'What did you call her?'

'What?'

'What did you call your mother?'

'I'm not sure.'

'Did you call her Mum? Or Mummy?'

'Oh. Mum, I suppose.'

'Mama?'

'I don't remember.'

But I do. The mouth sound comes to me now, sitting in the bush with the smell of hot banana around me. I feel it forming in my throat, how my mouth and lips make the shape to contain and hold it, how I almost draw the sound back into me, like milk. Embarrassing, even here, in the night. Even to mouth it. (Mama.) I feel the cushion of my lips, allow the sound to escape in tiny bursts, puffs of moist air, placid, experimental. She is mine.

Acknowledgments

This book was written with the help of a mentorship, fellowship and numerous stays at the wonderful Varuna writers' centre. My thanks to the staff and fellow writers, the Dark family for housing me, Sheila Atkinson for feeding me, and especially Peter Bishop without whose faith, insights and encouragement it is hard to imagine this book existing.

Thanks to my agent, Jenny Darling, who believed in the manuscript. To the team at Text Publishing, Michael Heyward for his enthusiasm and for taking the risk, Chong for his beautiful cover, my publicist Bridie Riordan and particularly my editor Mandy Brett for her advocacy and craft, and whose acute suggestions have greatly enriched the book. Thanks also to Melanie Ostell for her counsel. And to Amanda Lohrey (who prompted me to throw away 60,000 words and begin again) for her encouragement and honesty.

I am grateful to the many friends and family members who have encouraged and listened over this project's long gestation. Particular thanks to those who have taken the time to read the manuscript in its various incarnations, and for their keen, perceptive comments: Sarah Boyd, Jennet Cole-Adams, Brigid Cole-Adams, Sophie Cunningham, Sieglinde Edward, Margaret Simons, Penelope Trevor.

There are many professionals who shared their time and expertise while I was researching stories on coma, anaesthesia and somatic disorders for the *Age* and *Sydney Morning Herald* newspapers, and whose ideas I have further plundered, synthesised and possibly distorted in the process of writing this novel. Particular thanks to Ted Freeman (and his book *The Catastrophe of Coma*), Kate Leslie and Enrico Cementon for filling in some gaps. Any inaccuracies are mine. Some of the ideas in this book I developed while reading Arnold Mindel's *Coma: The Dreambody Near Death*— again, I don't claim to have faithfully represented his ideas or methods.

Warm thanks also to somatic therapist Hendrika van Dyk for her valuable lessons, and to her teacher Julie Henderson, some of whose exercises I have adapted for this book. Big thanks also to John Brock for his steadfast support over many years.

My love and gratitude go finally to Peter Kenneally for his shrewd, delicate appraisals and for making me laugh. And to my children—my son, Finn, who opened my heart, and my daughter, Frannie, who did it again—without whom none of it would make sense.